MURDER IN THE FALLING SNOW

ALSO AVAILABLE

Murder in Midsummer
Murder Takes a Holiday
Murder by the Seaside
Murder at Christmas
Murder Under the Christmas Tree
Murder on Christmas Eve
Murder in Midwinter
Murder on a Winter's Night

MURDER IN THE FALLING SNOW

TEN CLASSIC CRIME STORIES

Edited by Cecily Gayford

Gladys Mitchell · Dorothy L. Sayers
R. Austin Freeman · Julian Symons
Edgar Wallace · Arthur Conan Doyle
L. T. Meade and Robert Eustace
Michael Innes · G. K. Chesterton
Ianthe Jerrold

P
PROFILE BOOKS

First published in Great Britain in 2022 by
PROFILE BOOKS LTD
29 Cloth Fair
London EC1A 7JQ
www.profilebooks.com

See p. 183 for individual stories' copyright information

1 3 5 7 9 10 8 6 4 2

Typeset in Fournier by MacGuru Ltd
Printed and bound in Great Britain by
CPI Group (UK) Ltd, Croydon CR0 4YY

A CIP catalogue record for this book is available from the British Library.

ISBN 978 1 80081 245 1
eISBN 978 1 80081 247 5

Contents

Haunted House

Gladys Mitchell

Seen through the window the landscape was wintry and bare. 'Better in spring,' said John Graham. He turned away from the window and looked at the fire of logs. 'But it's cosy enough in here. How do you like it, Morag?'

'I like it very well,' his wife replied, 'but you did not tell me it was haunted.'

'Haunted? Who said so?'

'It was the agent. He said it was nothing to hurt.'

'Oh that!' Her husband laughed it off. 'It was just his nonsense. You've been seeing too much of him, Morag. He did say something to me. Just sounds, he said, as one gets in any old house.'

'Yes, John, but what about the footprints?'

John Graham frowned.

'If you don't think you'll be happy here—' he began. But she laughed and called him her darling and said that she liked the house well.

*

One day Morag broached the subject of the haunting to the agent when he came for the rent.

He denied the rumours hotly, but admitted that the house had a bad name in the neighbourhood.

'But maybe folk have been frightened,' she suggested.

'Well, I don't know about that,' he answered, accepting the hint. 'What are a few odd noises? There's no danger, I can assure you.' He got up to go, but she detained him.

'Francis, I know you won't deceive me. Have you heard anything yourself?'

He hesitated; then he answered.

'Twice, but it didn't amount to much. Just noises and something that sounded like footsteps, you know.'

'What about the footprints splashed with blood?'

'I never heard of any such thing, nor saw it, either. It's old wives' tales you've been hearing.'

Time passed, spring drew near and the agent became a less frequent visitor. Nothing ghostly was seen or heard.

Then rumour began again. The village at that time of the year had little to gossip about, so it continued to remark upon the number of times the agent still visited the house, and to speculate, not too kindly, upon the reason.

The gossip was kept from Morag this time, but between her and her husband something hovered in the air, something intangible, invisible and silent.

She proposed that they should give a little party to the half-dozen friends they had made. He agreed – heavily, she thought.

But the party was not a success.

When the first guests left, it was snowing. Between the black of the night and the glow from the house the large flakes swirled and melted, spinning like stars or softly falling like leaves. Huddling their coats against the snowfall, the departing guests stole away, themselves no more than ghosts as the snow settled down on their shoulders.

At last only one guest was left, the agent, Francis. At half-past eleven he, too, declared that he must go. He went for his coat and scarf. Graham went to the front and looked out. The snow was already in drift and was falling faster than before.

Graham withdrew from the door, closed it and put his back against it. When Francis came into the hall he said in belligerent tones:

'You'll never reach home. You'll never get through tonight. You'd better have our room. Morag can sleep in the warm down here on the settee, and I have a camp bed I use when I come in late.'

The house, supposed to be haunted, had no near neighbours, so that no one except the three who slept there that night could say when the sounds began. They had retired at just after midnight – both witnesses were agreed upon that. But after that their stories varied, although they were taken over them time and again. One man, the police decided, was lying, and the other was telling the truth.

Graham told the sergeant in charge that he had found Morag, his wife, dead on the dining-room floor when he went to call her in the morning. She had been sleeping in the drawing room on the settee.

He had rushed out for the village doctor, hoping against hope that something could be done. Morag Graham had been stabbed and had been dead for several hours by the time the doctor arrived. Graham had then collapsed, and Francis had run for the police.

Later, when the police had seen and photographed the body and the room in which it had been found, and had taken fingerprints and looked for clues, Graham told his full story.

He said that the three of them – himself, Morag and Francis, had separated at just after midnight, and that Morag had had a cup of cocoa and the two men had each drunk a nightcap of whisky and water. As it had proved impossible for Francis to get home that night, he had been offered a bed.

Graham knew no more until he had gone to wake his wife and suggest that it was time for a cup of tea and breakfast. He had found her stabbed in the back, her progress from the drawing room being marked by her own bloodstained footprints.

'You think, then,' said the inspector, 'that your wife was attacked in the drawing room, staggered into the dining room and there collapsed and died?'

Graham did think so, and appeared to be deeply affected.

The police then asked Francis for a statement. He gave substantially the same account as Graham had done, except for one particular. He had been awakened, he alleged, at about four in the morning by sounds which he could not interpret.

Asked to describe the sounds, he said that they resembled scuffling and moaning. He had lighted his bedside candle and had sat up to listen. He had also looked at his watch.

'How long did the sounds continue?' he was asked.

'About three or four minutes, but it might have been longer.'

'Why didn't you go and investigate?'

'I knew the house was said to be haunted, so I didn't bother.'

'Didn't it occur to you that one of the Grahams might have been taken ill?'

'No, it never occurred to me, and if it had, I should have thought it no business of mine as there would have been the other one there.'

'What happened after that?'

'Nothing, so far as I know. I just lay down and went to sleep again. We'd had rather a lot to drink during the evening so I may still have been a bit fuddled.'

'I see. Now what about these sleeping arrangements. Who made them?'

'It was Graham himself.'

'Not Mrs Graham?'

'Well, they may have talked it over in the kitchen. I wouldn't know about that. It was certainly Graham who mentioned them to me.'

'Didn't they seem to you rather peculiar?'

'Yes, but it wasn't any business of mine.'

Graham was recalled.

'Who decided that Francis should occupy the double bed?'

'My wife and I agreed about it. Francis was a wee bit drunk and we thought maybe he would tumble out of the camp bed or off the settee. We didn't want that. It would have frightened my wife.'

'Better be frightened than dead,' thought the officer grimly, but naturally did not give voice to this opinion. There seemed no other evidence available.

The medical evidence agreed well enough with the time given by Francis, and the snow had ceased at just after two in the morning, so that it was clear that no stranger had approached the house.

All the footprints in the snow could be identified as being those of the two men and the police. It was a curious and baffling case. Even the weapon did not help.

Mrs Graham had been stabbed with a Zulu assegai which had been hanging on the drawing-room wall. It had been wiped clear of fingerprints and hung up again, and it was sufficiently long for the murderer to have avoided getting blood on his clothing, although both men's garments had been meticulously examined.

'Well, there it is,' said the inspector to the Chief Constable.

'One of them did it, sir, and of course there's no trouble about the motive. It's a sex crime all right. There appears to have been a rare lot of gossip about it in the village – the affair between Mrs Graham and Francis, I mean.

'Personally, I'd put my money on Graham. He seems to have had a lot to put up with, if rumour can be believed. But there's no actual evidence one way or the other so far as I can see. You can't hang a man on probability only. The only thing I can suggest is to arrest them both, charge them jointly, and let the magistrates sort it out.'

'You know, it's that arrangement about the sleeping that puzzles me,' said the Chief Constable. 'I mean, is it reasonable to hand over the only comfortable bed in the house to a man guest and expect your wife to sleep on the settee?'

'It may have been the wife's arrangement, you know, sir.'

'Yes, there's that, of course. I wonder why she made for the dining room when she was attacked? And why there was no blood on the settee?'

'I don't know, sir.'

'I wonder whether we ought to attach any importance to the fact that none of the three could have known beforehand that Francis was going to stay the night?'

'I don't really think so, sir. One of them suddenly saw an opportunity and seized it. I should say. And, of course, they were both pretty drunk, apparently, and men will do things under the influence which normally they wouldn't think of doing, however much they might secretly want to.'

'That's true enough, but it doesn't help us if they were both drunk. It means it's as long as it's broad. Let's go over it again. There might be something we've overlooked. Yes! By Jove! I think we've got him! Have him in again.'

Graham looked haggard but defiant.

'Can't you leave me alone?' he asked. 'I've told you over and over again that I don't know anything more.'

'I'm going to tell you, not ask you, this time,' said the

Chief Constable. 'I'll tell you exactly what happened. You can correct me if I go wrong.

'I suggest that you deliberately arranged the sleeping so that you could confirm your suspicions of your wife and Francis. You thought she would take the risk of going to him in that double bed. Instead of going to the camp bed you sneaked into the kitchen from where you could keep track of the proceedings.

'Your suspicions proved to be well-founded. As soon as your wife rose from the settee you rushed in and snatched down the assegai. She fled from you – not up the stairs (for she realised that that would not save her) but into the dining room where she hoped to be able to slam the door on you. You were a little too quick for her.

'I'm sorry for you, Graham, but the officer must make his arrest. She *must* have got up off that settee, for there was no blood on it.'

This reasoning broke Graham down.

'There's one thing, sir,' said the inspector soberly. Whether that house was haunted before this happened I wouldn't really care to say, but I reckon it's haunted now.'

Sleuths on the Scent

Dorothy L. Sayers

The commercial room at the Pig and Pewter presented to Mr Montague Egg the aspect of a dim cavern in which some primaeval inhabitant had been cooking his mammoth-meat over a fire of damp seaweed. In other words, it was ill lit, cold, smoky, and permeated with an odour of stale food.

'Oh dear, oh dear!' muttered Mr Egg. He poked at the sullen coals, releasing a volume of pea-coloured smoke which made him cough.

Mr Egg rang the bell.

'Oh, if you please, sir,' said the maid who answered the summons, 'I'm sure I'm very sorry, but it's always this way when the wind's in the east, sir, and we've tried ever so many sorts of cowls and chimney-pots, you'd be surprised. The man was here today a-working in it, which is why the fire wasn't lit till just now, sir, but they don't seem able to do nothink with it. But there's a beautiful fire in the bar-parlour, sir, if you cared to step along. There's a very pleasant party in there, sir. I'm sure you would be comfortable. There's another commercial gentleman like yourself, sir, and old Mr Faggott and Sergeant Jukes over from Drabblesford. Oh, and there's two parties of motorists, but they're all quite nice and quiet, sir.'

'That'll suit me all right,' said Mr Egg amiably. But he made a mental note, nevertheless, that he would warn his fellow-commercials against the Pig and Pewter at Mugbury, for an inn is judged by its commercial room. Moreover, the dinner had been bad, with a badness not to be explained by his own rather late arrival.

In the bar-parlour, however, things were better. At one side of the cheerful hearth sat old Mr Faggott, an aged countryman, beneath whose scanty white beard dangled a long, scarlet comforter. In his hand was a tankard of ale. Opposite to him, also with a tankard, was a large man, obviously a policeman in mufti. At a table in front of the fireplace sat an alert-looking, darkish, youngish man whom Mr Egg instantly identified as the commercial gentleman by the stout leather bag at his side. He was drinking sherry. A young man and a girl in motorcycling kit were whispering together at another table, over a whisky-and-polly and a glass of port. Another man, with his hat and burberry on, was ordering Guinness at the little serving-hatch which communicated with the bar, while, in a far corner, an indeterminate male figure sat silent and half concealed by a slouch hat and a newspaper. Mr Egg saluted the company with respect and observed that it was a nasty night.

The commercial gentleman uttered an emphatic agreement.

'I ought to have got on to Drabblesford tonight,' he added, 'but with this frost and drizzle and frost again the roads are in such a state, I think I'd better stay where I am.'

'Same here,' said Mr Egg, approaching the hatch. 'Half of mild-and-bitter, please. Cold, too, isn't it?'

'Very cold,' said the policeman.

'Ar,' said old Mr Faggott.

'Foul,' said the man in the burberry, returning from the hatch and seating himself near the commercial gentleman. 'I've reason to know it. Skidded into a telegraph-pole two miles out. You should see my bumpers. Well! I suppose it's only to be expected this time of year.'

'Ar!' said old Mr Faggott. There was a pause.

'Well,' said Mr Egg, politely raising his tankard, 'here's luck!'

The company acknowledged the courtesy in a suitable manner, and another pause followed. It was broken by the traveller.

'Acquainted with this part of the country, sir?'

'Why, no,' said Monty Egg. 'It's not my usual beat. Bastable covers it as a rule – Henry Bastable – perhaps you know him? He and I travel for Plummet & Rose, Wines and Spirits.'

'Tall, red-haired fellow?'

'That's him. Laid up with rheumatic fever, poor chap, so I'm taking over temporarily. My name's Egg – Montague Egg.'

'Oh, yes, I think I've heard of you from Taylor of

Harrogate Bros. Redwood is my name. Fragonard & Co., perfumes and toilet accessories.'

Mr Egg bowed and inquired, in a discreet and general way, how Mr Redwood was finding things.

'Not too bad. Of course, money's a bit tight; that's only to be expected. But, considering everything, not too bad. I've got a line here, by the way, which is doing pretty well and may give *you* something to think about.' He bent over, unstrapped his bag and produced a tall flask, its glass stopper neatly secured with a twist of fine string. 'Tell me what you think of that.' He removed the string and handed the sample to Monty.

'Parma violet?' said that gentleman, with a glance at the label. 'The young lady should be the best judge of this. Allow me, miss. Sweets to the sweet,' he added gallantly. 'You'll excuse me, I'm sure.'

The girl giggled.

'Go on, Gert,' said her companion. 'Never refuse a good offer.' He removed the stopper and sniffed heartily at the perfume. 'This is high-class stuff, this is. Put a drop on your handkerchief. Here – I'll do it for you!'

'Oh! It's lovely!' said the girl. 'Refined, I call it. Get along, Arthur, do! Leave my handkerchief alone – what they'll all think of you! I'm sure this gentleman won't mind you having a drop for yourself if you want it.'

Arthur favoured the company with a large wink, and sprinkled his handkerchief liberally. Monty rescued the flask and passed it to the man in the burberry.

'Excuse me, sir,' said Mr Redwood, 'but if I might point it out, it's not everybody knows the right way to test perfume.

Just dab a little on the hand, wait while the liquid evaporates, and then raise the hand to the nostrils.'

'Like this?' said the man in the burberry, dexterously hitching the stopper out with his little finger, pouring a drop of perfume into his left palm, and re-stoppering the bottle, all in one movement. 'Yes, I see what you mean.'

'That's very interesting,' said Monty, much impressed and following the example set him. 'Same as when you put old brandy in a thin glass and cradle it in the hollow of the palm to bring out the aroma. The warmth of the hand makes the ethers expand. I'm very glad to know from you, Mr Redwood, what is the correct method with perfumes. Ready to learn means ready to earn – that's Monty Egg, every time. A very fine perfume indeed. Would you like to try it, sir?'

He offered the bottle first to the aged countryman (who shook his head, remarking acidly that he 'couldn't abide smells and sich nastiness') and then to the policeman, who, disdaining refinements, took a strong sniff at the bottle and pronounced the scent 'good, but a bit powerful for his liking'.

'Well, well, tastes differ,' said Monty. He glanced round, and, observing the silent man in the far corner, approached him confidently with a request for his opinion.

'What the devil's the matter with *you*?' growled this person, emerging reluctantly from behind his barricade of newspaper, and displaying a bristling and bellicose fair moustache and a pair of sulky blue eyes. 'There seems to be no peace in this bar. Scent? Can't abide the stuff.' He snatched the perfume impatiently from Mr Egg's hand, sniffed, and thrust the stopper back with such blind and fumbling haste that it missed the neck of the flask altogether and rolled away ıder the table. 'Well, it's scent. What else do you want me to say about it? I'm not going to buy it, if that's what you're after.'

'Certainly not, sir,' said Mr Redwood, hurt, and hastening to retrieve his scattered property. 'Wonder what's bitten him,' he continued, in a confidential undertone. 'Nasty glitter in his eye. Hands all of a tremble. Better look out for him, sergeant. We don't want murder done. Well, anyhow, madam and gentlemen, what should you say if I was to tell you that we're able to retail that large bottle, as it stands – retail it, mind you – at three shillings and sixpence?'

'Three-and-six?' said Mr Egg, surprised. 'Why, I should have thought that wouldn't so much as pay the duty on the spirit.'

'Nor it would,' triumphed Mr Redwood, 'if it was spirit. But it isn't, and that's the whole point. It's a trade secret and I can't say more, but if you were to be asked whether that was or was not the finest Parma violet, equal to the most expensive marks, I don't mind betting you'd never know the difference.'

'No, indeed,' said Mr Egg. 'Wonderful, I call it. Pity they can't discover something similar to help the wine and spirit business, though I needn't say it wouldn't altogether do, or what would the Chancellor of the Exchequer have to say about it? Talking of that, what are you drinking? And you, miss? I hope you'll allow me, gentlemen. Same again all round, please.'

The landlord hastened to fulfil the order and, as he passed through the bar-parlour, switched on the wireless, which instantly responded with the nine o'clock time-signal, followed clearly by the voice of the announcer:

'This is the National programme from London. Before I read the weather report, here is a police message. In connection with the murder of Alice Steward, at Nottingham, we are asked by the Commissioner of Police to broadcast the following. The police are anxious to get in touch with a young man named Gerald Beeton, who is known to have visited the deceased on the afternoon preceding her death. This man is aged thirty-five, medium height, medium build, fair hair, small moustache, grey or blue eyes, full face, fresh colour. When last seen was wearing a grey lounge suit, soft grey hat, and fawn overcoat, and is thought to be now travelling the country in a Morris car, number unknown. Will this man, or anyone able to throw light on his whereabouts, please communicate at once with the Superintendent of Police, Nottingham, or with any police station ? Here is the weather report. A deep depression …'

'Oh, switch it off, George,' urged Mr Redwood. 'We don't want to hear about depressions.'

'That's right,' agreed the landlord, switching off. 'What gets me is these police descriptions. How'd they think anyone's going to recognise a man from the sort of stuff they give you? Medium this and medium the other, and ordinary face and fair complexion and a soft hat – might be anybody.'

'So it might,' said Monty. 'It might be me.'

'Well, that's true, it might,' said Mr Redwood. 'Or it might be this gentleman.'

'That's a fact,' admitted the man in the burberry. 'Or it might be fifty men out of every hundred.'

'Yes, or' – Monty jerked his head cautiously towards the newspaper in the corner – 'him!'

'Well, so you say,' said Redwood, 'but nobody else has seen him to look at. Unless it's George.'

'I wouldn't care to swear to him,' said the landlord, with a smile. 'He come straight in here and ordered a drink and paid for it without so much as looking at me, but from what I did see of him the description would fit him as well as anybody. And what's more, he's got a Morris car – it's in the garage now.'

'That's nothing against him,' said Monty. 'So've I.'

'And I,' said the man in the burberry.

'And I,' chimed in Redwood. 'Encourage home industries, I say. But it's no help to identifying a man. Beg your pardon, sergeant, and all that, but why don't the police make it a bit easier for the public?'

'Why,' said the sergeant, 'because they 'as to rely on the damnfool description given to them by the public. That's why.'

'One up to you,' said Redwood pleasantly. 'Tell me, sergeant, all this stuff about wanting to interview the fellow is all eyewash, isn't it? I mean, what they really want to do is arrest him.'

'That ain't for me to say,' replied the sergeant ponderously. 'You must use your own judgment about that. What they're asking for is an interview, him being known to have been one of the last people to see her before she was done in. If he's sensible, he'll turn up. If he don't answer to the summons – well, you can think what you like.'

'Who is he, anyway?' asked Monty.

'Now you want to know something. Ain't you seen the evening papers?'

'No; I've been on the road since five o'clock.'

'Well, it's like this here. This old lady, Miss Alice Steward, lived all alone with a maid in a little 'ouse on the outskirts of Nottingham. Yesterday afternoon was the maid's afternoon out, and just as she was stepping out of the door, a bloke drives up in a Morris – or so *she* says, though you can't trust these girls, and if you ask me, it may just as well have been an Austin or Wolseley, or anything else, for that matter. He asks to see Miss Steward and the girl shows him into the sitting room, and as she does so she hears the old girl say, "Why, Gerald!" – like that. Well, she goes off to the pictures and leaves 'em to it, and when she gets back at ten o'clock, she finds the old lady lying with 'er 'ead bashed in.'

Mr Redwood leaned across and nudged Mr Egg. The stranger in the far corner had ceased to read his paper, and was peering stealthily round the edge of it.

'That's brought *him* to life, anyway,' muttered Mr Redwood. 'Well, sergeant, but how did the girl know the fellow's surname and who he was?'

'Why,' replied the sergeant, 'she remembered once 'earing the old lady speak of a man called Gerald Beeton – a good many years ago, or so she said, and she couldn't tell us much about it. Only she remembered the name, because it was the same as the one on her cookery-book.'

'Was that at Lewes?' demanded the young man called Arthur suddenly.

'Might have been,' admitted the sergeant, glancing rather sharply at him. 'The old lady came from Lewes. Why?'

'I remember, when I was a kid at school, hearing my mother mention an old Miss Steward at Lewes, who was very rich and had adopted a young fellow out of a chemist's shop. I think he ran away, and turned out badly, or something. Anyway, the old lady left the town. She was supposed to be very rich and to keep all her money in a tin box, or something. My mother's cousin knew an old girl who was Miss Steward's housekeeper – but I dare say it was all rot. Anyhow, that was about six or seven years ago, and I believe my mother's cousin is dead now and the housekeeper too. My mother,' went on the young man called Arthur, anticipating the next question, 'died two years ago.'

'That's very interesting, all the same,' said Mr Egg encouragingly. 'You ought to tell the police about it.'

'Well, I have, haven't I?' said Arthur, with a grin, indicating the sergeant. 'Though I expect they know it already. Or do I have to go to the police station?'

'For the present purpose,' replied the sergeant, 'I am a police station. But you might give me your name and address.'

The young man gave his name as Arthur Bunce, with an address in London. At this point the girl Gertrude was struck with an idea.

'But what about the tin box? D'you think he killed her to get it?'

'There's been nothing in the papers about the tin box,' put in the man in the burberry.

'They don't let everything get into the papers,' said the sergeant.

'It doesn't seem to be in the paper our disagreeable friend is reading,' murmured Mr Redwood, and as he spoke, that person rose from his seat and came over to the serving-hatch, ostensibly to order more beer, but with the evident intention of overhearing more of the conversation.

'I wonder if they'll catch the fellow,' pursued Redwood thoughtfully. 'They – by Jove! yes, that explains it – they must be keeping a pretty sharp lookout. I wondered why they held me up outside Wintonbury to examine my driving licence. I suppose they're checking all the Morrises on the roads. Some job.'

'All the Morrises in this district, anyway,' said Monty. 'They held me up just outside Thugford.'

'Oho!' cried Arthur Bunce, 'that looks as though they've got a line on the fellow. Now, sergeant, come across with it. What do you know about this, eh?'

'I can't tell you anything about that,' replied Sergeant Jukes, in a stately manner. The disagreeable man moved away from the serving-hatch, and at the same moment the sergeant rose and walked over to a distant table to knock out his pipe, rather unnecessarily, into a flowerpot. He remained there, refilling the pipe from his pouch, his bulky form towering between the Disagreeable Man and the door.

'They'll never catch him,' said the Disagreeable Man, suddenly and unexpectedly. 'They'll never catch him. And do you know why? I'll tell you. Not because he's too clever for them, but because he's too stupid. It's all too ordinary. I don't suppose it was this man Beeton at all. Don't you read your papers? Didn't you see that the old lady's sitting room was on the ground floor, and that the dining-room window was found open at the top? It would be the easiest thing in the world for a man to slip in through the dining room – Miss Steward was rather deaf – and catch her unawares and bash her on the head. There's only crazy paving between the garden gate and the windows, and there was a black frost yesterday night, so he'd leave no footmarks on the carpet. That's the difficult sort of murder to trace – no subtlety, no apparent motive. Look at the Reading murder, look at—'

'Hold hard a minute, sir,' interrupted the sergeant. 'How do you know there was crazy paving? *That's* not in the papers, as far as I know.'

The Disagreeable Man stopped short in the full tide of his eloquence, and appeared disconcerted.

'I've seen the place, as a matter of fact,' he said with some reluctance. 'Went there this morning to look at it – for private reasons, which I needn't trouble you with.'

'That's a funny thing to do, sir.'

'It may be, but it's no business of yours.'

'Oh, no, sir, of course not,' said the sergeant. 'We all of us has our little 'obbies, and crazy paving may be yours. Landscape gardener, sir?'

'Not exactly.'

'A journalist, perhaps?' suggested Mr Redwood.

'That's nearer,' said the other. 'Looking at my three fountain pens, eh? Quite the amateur detective.'

'The gentleman can't be a journalist,' said Mr Egg. 'You will pardon me, sir, but a journalist couldn't help but take an interest in Mr Redwood's synthetic alcohol or whatever it is. I fancy I might put a name to your profession if I was called upon to do so. Every man carries the marks of his trade, though it's not always as conspicuous as Mr Redwood's sample case or mine. Take books, for instance. I always know an academic gentleman by the way he opens a book.

It's in his blood, as you might say. Or take bottles. I handle them one way – it's my trade. A doctor or a chemist handles them another way. This scent-bottle, for example. If you or I was to take the stopper out of this bottle, how would we do it? How would you do it, Mr Redwood?'

'Me?' said Mr Redwood. 'Why, dash it all! On the word "one" I'd apply the thumb and two fingers of the right hand *to* the stopper and on the word "two" I would elevate them briskly, retaining a firm grip on the bottle with the left hand in case of accident. What would you do?' He turned to the man in the burberry.

'Same as you,' said that gentleman, suiting the action to the word. 'I don't see any difficulty about that. There's only one way I know of to take out stoppers, and that's to take 'em out. What d'you expect me to do? Whistle 'em out?'

'But this gentleman's quite right, all the same,' put in the Disagreeable Man. 'You do it that way because you aren't accustomed to measuring and pouring with one hand while the other's occupied. But a doctor or a chemist pulls the stopper out with his little finger, like this, and lifts the bottle in the same hand, holding the measuring-glass in his left – so – and when he—'

'Hi! Beeton!' cried Mr Egg in a shrill voice, 'look out!'

The flask slipped from the hand of the Disagreeable Man and crashed on the table's edge as the man in the burberry started to his feet. An overpowering odour of violets filled the room. The sergeant darted forward – there was a brief but violent struggle. The girl screamed. The landlord rushed in from the bar, and a crowd of men surged in after him and blocked the doorway.

'There,' said the sergeant, emerging a little breathless from the mix-up, 'you best come quiet. Wait a minute! Gotter charge you. Gerald Beeton, I arrest you for the murder of Alice Steward – stand still, can't you? – and I warns you as anything you say may be taken down and used in evidence at your trial. Thank you, sir. If you'll give me a 'and with him to the door, I've got a pal waiting just up the road, with a police car.'

In a few minutes' time Sergeant Jukes returned, struggling into his overcoat. His amateur helpers accompanied him, their faces bright, as of those who have done their good deed for the day.

'That was a very neat dodge of yours, sir,' said the sergeant, addressing Mr Egg, who was administering a stiff pick-me-up to the young lady, while Mr Redwood and the landlord together sought to remove the drench of Parma violet from the carpet. 'Whew! Smells a bit strong, don't it? Regular barber's shop. We had the office he was expected this way, and I had an idea that one of you gentlemen might be the man, but I didn't know which. Mr Bunce here saying that Beeton had been a chemist was a big help; and you, sir, I must say you touched him off proper.'

'Not at all,' said Mr Egg. 'I noticed the way he took that stopper out the first time – it showed he had been trained to laboratory work. That might have been an accident, of course. But afterwards, when he pretended he didn't know the right way to do it, I thought it was time to see if he'd answer to his name.'

'Good wheeze,' said the Disagreeable Man agreeably. 'Mind if I use it some time?'

'Ah!' said Sergeant Jukes. 'You gave me a bit of a turn, sir, with that crazy paving. Whatever did you—'

'Professional curiosity,' said the other, with a grin. 'I write detective stories. But our friend Mr Egg is a better hand at the real thing.'

'No, no,' said Monty. 'We all helped. The hardest problem's easy of solution when each one makes his little contribution. Isn't that so, Mr Faggott?'

The aged countryman had risen to his feet.

'Place fair stinks o' that dratted stuff,' he said disapprovingly. 'I can't abide such nastiness.' He hobbled out and shut the door.

Mr Ponting's Alibi

R. Austin Freeman

Thorndyke looked doubtfully at the pleasant-faced athletic-looking clergyman who had just come in, bearing Mr Brodribb's card as an explanatory credential.

'I don't quite see,' said he, 'why Mr Brodribb sent you to me. It seems to be a purely legal matter which he could have dealt with himself, at least as well as I can.'

'He appeared to think otherwise,' said the clergyman. ('The Revd. Charles Meade' was written on the card.)

'At any rate,' he added with a persuasive smile, 'here I am, and I hope you are not going to send me away.'

'I shouldn't offer that affront to my old friend Brodribb,' replied Thorndyke, smiling in return; 'so we may as well get to business, which, in the first place, involves the setting out of all the particulars. Let us begin with the lady who is the subject of the threats of which you spoke.'

'Her name,' said Mr Meade, 'is Miss Millicent Fawcett.

She is a person of independent means, which she employs in works of charity. She was formerly a hospital sister, and she does a certain amount of voluntary work in the parish as a sort of district nurse. She has been a very valuable help to me and we have been close friends for several years; and I may add, as a very material fact, that she has consented to marry me in about two months' time. So that, you see, I am properly entitled to act on her behalf.'

'Yes,' agreed Thorndyke. 'You are an interested party. And now, as to the threats. What do they amount to?'

'That,' replied Meade, 'I can't tell you. I gathered quite by chance, from some words that she dropped, that she had been threatened. But she was unwilling to say more on the subject, as she did not take the matter seriously. She is not at all nervous. However, I told her I was taking advice; and I hope you will be able to extract more details from her. For my own part, I am decidedly uneasy.'

'And as to the person or persons who have uttered the threats. Who are they? And out of what circumstances have the threats arisen?'

'The person is a certain William Ponting, who is Miss Fawcett's stepbrother – if that is the right term. Her father married, as his second wife, a Mrs Ponting, a widow with one son. This is the son. His mother died before Mr Fawcett, and the latter, when he died, left his daughter, Millicent, sole heir to his property. That has always been a grievance to Ponting. But now he has another. Miss Fawcett made a will some years ago by which the bulk of her rather considerable property is left to two cousins, Frederick and James Barnett, the sons of her father's sister. A comparatively small amount goes to Ponting. When he heard this he was furious. He demanded a portion at least equal to the others, and has continued to make this demand from time to time. In fact, he has been extremely troublesome, and appears to be getting still more so. I gathered that the threats were due to her refusal to alter the will.'

'But,' said I, 'doesn't he realise that her marriage will render that will null and void?'

'Apparently not,' replied Meade; 'nor, to tell the truth, did I realise it myself. Will she have to make a new will?'

'Certainly,' I replied. 'And as that new will may be expected to be still less favourable to him, that will presumably be a further grievance.'

'One doesn't understand,' said Thorndyke, 'why he should excite himself so much about her will. What are their respective ages?'

'Miss Fawcett is thirty-six and Ponting is about forty.'

'And what kind of man is he?' Thorndyke asked.

'A very unpleasant kind of man, I am sorry to say. Morose, rude and violent-tempered. A spendthrift and a cadger. He has had quite a lot of money from Miss Fawcett – loans, which, of course, are never repaid. And he is none too industrious, though he has a regular job on the staff of a weekly paper. But he seems to be always in debt.'

'We may as well note his address,' said Thorndyke.

'He lives in a small flat in Bloomsbury – alone now, since he quarrelled with the man who used to share it with him. The address is 12 Borneo House, Devonshire Street.'

'What sort of terms is he on with the cousins, his rivals?'

'No sort of terms now,' replied Meade. 'They used to be

great friends. So much so that he took his present flat to be near them – they live in the adjoining flat, number 12 Sumatra House. But since the trouble about the wills he is hardly on speaking terms with them.'

'They live together, then?'

'Yes, Frederick and his wife and James, who is unmarried. They are rather a queer lot, too. Frederick is a singer on the variety stage, and James accompanies him on various instruments. But they are both sporting characters of a kind, especially James, who does a bit on the turf and engages in other odd activities. Of course, their musical habits are a grievance to Ponting. He is constantly making complaints of their disturbing him at his work.'

Mr Meade paused and looked wistfully at Thorndyke, who was making full notes of the conversation.

'Well,' said the latter, 'we seem to have got all the facts excepting the most important – the nature of the threats. What do you want us to do?'

'I want you to see Miss Fawcett – with me, if possible – and induce her to give you such details as would enable you to put a stop to the nuisance. You couldn't come tonight, I suppose? It is a beast of a night, but I would take you there in a taxi – it is only to Tooting Bec. What do you say?' he added eagerly, as Thorndyke made no objection. 'We are sure to find her in, because her maid is away on a visit to her home and she is alone in the house.'

Thorndyke looked reflectively at his watch.

'Half-past eight,' he remarked, 'and half an hour to get there. These threats are probably nothing but ill-temper. But we don't know. There may be something more serious behind them; and, in law as in medicine, prevention is better than a post-mortem. What do you say, Jervis?'

What could I say? I would much sooner have sat by the fire with a book than turn out into the murk of a November night. But I felt it necessary, especially as Thorndyke had evidently made up his mind. Accordingly I made a virtue of necessity; and a couple of minutes later we had exchanged the cosy room for the chilly darkness of Inner Temple Lane, up which the gratified parson was speeding ahead to capture a taxi. At the top of the Lane we perceived him giving elaborate instructions to a taxi driver as he held the door of the cab open; and Thorndyke, having carefully disposed of his research-case – which, to my secret amusement, he had caught up, from mere force of habit, as we started – took his seat, and Meade and I followed.

As the taxi trundled smoothly along the dark streets, Mr Meade filled in the details of his previous sketch, and, in a simple, manly, unaffected way dilated upon his good fortune and the pleasant future that lay before him. It was not, perhaps, a romantic marriage, he admitted; but Miss Fawcett and he had been faithful friends for years, and faithful friends they would remain till death did them part. So he ran on, now gleefully, now with a note of anxiety, and we listened by no means unsympathetically, until at last the cab drew up at a small, unpretentious house, standing in its own little grounds in a quiet suburban road.

'She is at home, you see,' observed Meade, pointing to a lighted ground-floor window. He directed the taxi driver to wait for the return journey, and striding up the path, delivered a characteristic knock at the door. As this brought no response, he knocked again and rang the bell. But still there was no answer, though twice I thought I heard the sound of a bolt being either drawn or shot softly. Again Mr Meade plied the knocker more vigorously, and pressed the push of the bell, which we could hear ringing loudly within.

'This is very strange,' said Meade, in an anxious tone, keeping his thumb pressed on the bell-push. 'She can't have gone out and left the electric light on. What had we better do?'

'We had better enter without more delay,' Thorndyke replied. 'There were certainly sounds from within. Is there a side gate?'

Meade ran off towards the side of the house, and Thorndyke and I glanced at the lighted window, which was slightly open at the top.

'Looks a bit queer,' I remarked, listening at the letterbox.

Thorndyke assented gravely, and at this moment Meade returned, breathing hard.

'The side gate is bolted inside,' said he; and at this I recalled the stealthy sound of the bolt that I had heard. 'What is to be done?'

Without replying, Thorndyke handed me his research-case, stepped across to the window, sprang up on the sill, drew down the upper sash and disappeared between the curtains into the room. A moment later the street door opened and Meade and I entered the hall. We glanced through the open doorway into the lighted room, and I noticed a heap of needlework thrown hastily on the dining table. Then Meade switched on the hall light, and Thorndyke walked quickly past him to the half-open door of the next room. Before entering, he reached in and switched on the light; and as he stepped into the room he partly closed the door behind him.

'Don't come in here, Meade!' he called out. But the parson's eye, like my own, had seen something before the door closed: a great, dark stain on the carpet just within the threshold. Regardless of the admonition, he pushed the door open and darted into the room. Following him, I saw him rush forward, fling his arms up wildly, and with a dreadful, strangled cry, sink upon his knees beside a low couch on which a woman was lying.

'Merciful God!' he gasped. 'She is dead! Is she dead, doctor? Can nothing be done?'

Thorndyke shook his head. 'Nothing,' he said in a low voice. 'She is dead.'

Poor Meade knelt by the couch, his hands clutching at his hair and his eyes riveted on the dead face, the very embodiment of horror and despair.

'God Almighty!' he exclaimed in the same strangled undertone. 'How frightful! Poor, poor Millie! Dear, sweet friend!' Then suddenly – almost savagely – he turned to Thorndyke. 'But it can't be, doctor! It is impossible – unbelievable. That, I mean!' and he pointed to the dead woman's right hand, which held an open razor.

Our poor friend had spoken my own thought. It was incredible that this refined, pious lady should have inflicted those savage wounds that gaped scarlet beneath the waxen face. There, indeed, was the razor lying in her hand. But what was its testimony worth? My heart rejected it; but yet, unwillingly, I noted that the wounds seemed to support it;

for they had been made from left to right, as they would have been if self-inflicted.

'It is hard to believe,' said Thorndyke, 'but there is only one alternative. Someone should acquaint the police at once.'

'I will go,' exclaimed Meade, starting up. 'I know the way and the cab is there.' He looked once more with infinite pity and affection at the dead woman. 'Poor, sweet girl!' he murmured. 'If we can do no more for you, we can defend your memory from calumny and call upon the God of Justice to right the innocent and punish the guilty.'

With these words and a mute farewell to his dead friend, he hurried from the room, and immediately afterwards we heard the street door close.

As he went out, Thorndyke's manner changed abruptly. He had been deeply moved – as who would not have been – by this awful tragedy that had in a moment shattered the happiness of the genial, kindly parson. Now he turned to me with a face set and stern. 'This is an abominable affair, Jervis,' he said in an ominously quiet voice.

'You reject the suggestion of suicide, then?' said I, with a feeling of relief that surprised me.

'Absolutely,' he replied. 'Murder shouts at us from everything that meets our eye. Look at this poor woman, in her trim nurse's dress, with her unfinished needlework lying on the table in the next room and that preposterous razor loose in her limp hand. Look at the savage wounds. Four of them, and the first one mortal. The great bloodstain by the door, the great bloodstain on her dress from the neck to the feet. The gashed collar, the cap-string cut right through. Note that the bleeding had practically ceased when she lay down. That is a group of visible facts that is utterly inconsistent with the idea of suicide. But we are wasting time. Let us search the premises thoroughly. The murderer has pretty certainly got away, but as he was in the house when we arrived, any traces will be quite fresh.'

As he spoke he took his electric lamp from the research-case and walked to the door.

'We can examine this room later,' he said, 'but we had better look over the house. If you will stay by the stairs and watch the front and back doors, I will look through the upper rooms.'

He ran lightly up the stairs while I kept watch below, but he was absent less than a couple of minutes.

'There is no one there,' he reported, 'and as there is no basement we will just look at this floor and then examine the grounds.'

After a rapid inspection of the ground-floor rooms, including the kitchen, we went out by the back door, which was unbolted, and inspected the grounds. These consisted of a largish garden with a small orchard at the side. In the former we could discover no traces of any kind, but at the end of the path that crossed the orchard we came to a possible clue. The orchard was enclosed by a five-foot fence, the top of which bristled with hooked nails; and at the point opposite to the path, Thorndyke's lantern brought into view one or two wisps of cloth caught on the hooks.

'Someone has been over here,' said Thorndyke, 'but as this is an orchard, there is nothing remarkable in the fact. However, there is no fruit on the trees now, and the cloth looks fairly fresh. There are two kinds, you notice: a dark blue and a black and white mixture of some kind.'

'Corresponding, probably, to the coat and trousers,' I suggested.

'Possibly,' he agreed, taking from his pocket a couple of the little seed-envelopes of which he always carried a supply. Very delicately he picked the tiny wisps of cloth from the hooks and bestowed each kind in a separate envelope. Having pocketed these, he leaned over the fence and threw the light of his lamp along the narrow lane or alley that divided the orchard from the adjoining premises. It was ungravelled and covered with a growth of rank grass, which suggested that it was little frequented. But immediately below was a small patch of bare earth, and on this was a very distinct impression of a foot, covering several less distinct prints.

'Several people have been over here at different times,' I remarked.

'Yes,' Thorndyke agreed. 'But that sharp footprint belongs to the last one over, and he is our concern. We had better not confuse the issues by getting over ourselves. We will mark the spot and explore from the other end.' He laid his handkerchief over the top of the fence and we then went back to the house.

'You are going to take a plaster cast, I suppose?' said I; and as he assented, I fetched the research-case from the drawing room. Then we fixed the catch of the front-door latch and went out, drawing the door to after us.

We found the entrance to the alley about sixty yards from the gate, and entering it, walked slowly forwards, scanning the ground as we went. But the bright lamplight showed nothing more than the vague marks of trampling feet on the grass until we came to the spot marked by the handkerchief on the fence.

'It is a pity,' I remarked, 'that this footprint has obliterated the others.'

'On the other hand,' he replied, 'this one, which is the one that interests us, is remarkably clear and characteristic: a circular heel and a rubber sole of a recognisable pattern mended with a patch of cement paste. It is a footprint that could be identified beyond a doubt.'

As he was speaking, he took from the research-case the water bottle, plaster tin, rubber mixing bowl and spoon, and a piece of canvas with which to 'reinforce' the cast. Rapidly, he mixed a bowlful – extra thick, so that it should set quickly and hard – dipped the canvas into it, poured the remainder into the footprint, and laid the canvas on it.

'I will get you to stay here, Jervis,' said he, 'until the plaster has set. I want to examine the body rather more thoroughly before the police arrive, particularly the back.'

'Why the back?' I asked.

'Did not the appearance of the body suggest to you the advisability of examining the back?' he asked, and then, without waiting for a reply, he went off, leaving the inspection-lamp with me.

His words gave me matter for profound thought during my short vigil. I recalled the appearance of the dead woman very vividly – indeed, I am not likely ever to forget it – and I strove to connect that appearance with his desire to examine the back of the corpse. But there seemed to be no connection at all. The visible injuries were in front, and I had seen nothing to suggest the existence of any others. From time to time I tested the condition of the plaster, impatient to rejoin my colleague but fearful of cracking the thin cast by raising it prematurely. At length the plaster seemed to be hard enough, and trusting to the strength of the canvas, I prised cautiously at the edge, when, to my relief, the brittle plate came up safely and I lifted it clear. Wrapping it carefully in some spare rag, I packed it in the research-case, and then, taking this and the lantern, made my way back to the house.

When I had let down the catch and closed the front door, I went to the drawing room, where I found Thorndyke stooping over the dark stain at the threshold and scanning the floor as if in search of something. I reported the completion of the cast and then asked him what he was looking for.

'I am looking for a button,' he replied. 'There is one missing from the back; the one to which the collar was fastened.'

'Is it of any importance?' I asked.

'It is important to ascertain when and where it became detached,' he replied. 'Let us have the inspection-lamp.'

I gave him the lamp, which he placed on the floor, turning it so that its beam of light travelled along the surface. Stooping to follow the light, I scrutinised the floor minutely but in vain.

'It may not be here at all,' said I; but at that moment the bright gleam, penetrating the darkness under a cabinet, struck a small object close to the wall. In a moment I had thrown myself prone on the carpet, and reaching under the cabinet, brought forth a largish mother-of-pearl button.

'You notice,' said Thorndyke, as he examined it, 'that the

cabinet is near the window, at the opposite end of the room to the couch. But we had better see that it is the right button.'

He walked slowly towards the couch, still stooping and searching the floor with the light. The corpse, I noticed, had been turned on its side, exposing the back and the displaced collar. Through the strained button-hole of the latter Thorndyke passed the button without difficulty.

'Yes,' he said, 'that is where it came from. You will notice that there is a similar one in front. By the way,' he continued, bringing the lamp close to the surface of the grey serge dress, 'I picked off one or two hairs – animal hairs; cat and dog they looked like. Here are one or two more. Will you hold the lamp while I take them off?'

'They are probably from some pets of hers,' I remarked, as he picked them off with his forceps and deposited them in one of the invaluable seed-envelopes. 'Spinsters are a good deal addicted to pets, especially cats and dogs.'

'Possibly,' he replied. 'But I could see none in front, where you would expect to find them, and there seem to be none on the carpet. Now let us replace the body as we found it and just have a look at our material before the police arrive. I expected them here before this.'

We turned the body back into its original position, and taking the research-case and the lamp, went into the dining room. Here Thorndyke rapidly set up the little travelling microscope, and bringing forth the seed-envelopes, began to prepare slides from the contents of some while I prepared the others. There was time only for a very hasty examination, which Thorndyke made as soon as the specimens were mounted.

'The clothing,' he reported, with his eye at the microscope, 'is woollen in both cases. Fairly good quality. The one a blue serge, apparently indigo-dyed; the other a mixture of black and white, no other colour. Probably a fine tabby or a small shepherd's plaid.'

'Serge coat and shepherd's plaid trousers,' I suggested. 'Now see what the hairs are.' I handed him the slide, on which I had roughly mounted the collection in oil of lavender, and he placed it on the stage.

'There are three different kinds of hairs here,' he reported, after a rapid inspection. 'Some are obviously from a cat – a smoky Persian. Others are long, rather fine tawny hairs from a dog. Probably a Pekinese. But there are two that I can't quite place. They look like monkey's hairs, but they are a very unusual colour. There is a perceptible greenish tint, which is extremely uncommon in mammalian hairs. But I hear the taxi approaching. We need not be expansive to the local police as to what we have observed. This will probably be a case for the CID.'

I went out into the hall and opened the door as Meade came up the path, followed by two men; and as the latter came into the light, I was astonished to recognise in one of them our old friend, Detective Superintendent Miller, the other being, apparently, the station superintendent.

'We have kept Mr Meade a long time,' said Miller, 'but we knew you were here, so the time wouldn't be wasted. Thought it best to get a full statement before we inspected the premises. How do, doctor?' he added, shaking hands with Thorndyke. 'Glad to see you here. I suppose you have got all the facts. I understood so from Mr Meade.'

'Yes,' replied Thorndyke, 'we have all the antecedents of the case, and we arrived within a few minutes of the death of the deceased.'

'Ha!' exclaimed Miller. 'Did you? And I expect you have formed an opinion on the question as to whether the injuries were self-inflicted?'

'I think,' said Thorndyke, 'that it would be best to act on the assumption that they were not – and to act promptly.'

'Precisely,' Miller agreed emphatically. 'You mean that we had better find out at once where a certain person was at— What time did you arrive here?'

'It was two minutes to nine when the taxi stopped,' replied Thorndyke; 'and, as it is now only twenty-five minutes to ten, we have good time if Mr Meade can spare us the taxi. I have the address.'

'The taxi is waiting for you,' said Mr Meade, 'and the man has been paid for both journeys. I shall stay here in case the superintendent wants anything.' He shook our hands warmly, and as we bade him farewell and noted the dazed, despairing expression and lines of grief that had already eaten into the face that had been so blithe and hopeful, we both thought bitterly of the few fatal minutes that had made us too late to save the wreckage of his life.

We were just turning away when Thorndyke paused and again faced the clergyman. 'Can you tell me,' he asked, 'whether Miss Fawcett had any pets? Cats, dogs, or other animals?'

Meade looked at him in surprise, and Superintendent Miller seemed to prick up his ears. But the former answered simply: 'No. She was not very fond of animals; she reserved her affections for men and women.'

Thorndyke nodded gravely, and picking up the research-case walked slowly out of the room, Miller and I following.

As soon as the address had been given to the driver and we had taken our seats in the taxi, the superintendent opened the examination-in-chief.

'I see you have got your box of magic with you, doctor,' he said, cocking his eye at the research-case. 'Any luck?'

'We have secured a very distinctive footprint,' replied Thorndyke, 'but it may have no connection with the case.'

'I hope it has,' said Miller. 'A good cast of a footprint which you can let the jury compare with the boot is first-class evidence.' He took the cast, which I had produced from the research-case, and turning it over tenderly and gloatingly, exclaimed: 'Beautiful! beautiful! Absolutely distinctive! There can't be another exactly like it in the world. It is as good as a fingerprint. For the Lord's sake take care of it. It means a conviction if we can find the boot.'

The superintendent's efforts to engage Thorndyke in discussion were not very successful, and the conversational brunt was borne by me. For we both knew my colleague too well to interrupt him if he was disposed to be meditative. And such was now his disposition. Looking at him as he sat in his corner, silent but obviously wrapped in thought, I knew that he was mentally sorting out the data and testing the hypotheses that they yielded.

'Here we are,' said Miller, opening the door as the taxi stopped. 'Now what are we going to say? Shall I tell him who I am?'

'I expect you will have to,' replied Thorndyke, 'if you want him to let us in.'

'Very well,' said Miller. 'But I shall let you do the talking, because I don't know what you have got up your sleeve.'

Thorndyke's prediction was verified literally. In response to the third knock, with an *obbligato* accompaniment on the bell, wrathful footsteps – I had no idea footsteps could be so expressive – advanced rapidly along the lobby, the door was wrenched open – but only for a few inches – and an angry, hairy face appeared in the opening.

'Now then,' the hairy person demanded, 'what the deuce do you want?'

'Are you Mr William Ponting?' the superintendent inquired.

'What the devil is that to do with you?' was the genial answer – in the Scottish mode.

'We have business,' Miller began persuasively.

'So have I,' the presumable Ponting replied, 'and mine won't wait.'

'But our business is very important,' Miller urged.

'So is mine,' snapped Ponting, and would have shut the door but for Miller's obstructing foot, at which he kicked viciously, but with unsatisfactory results, as he was shod in light slippers, whereas the superintendent's boots were of constabulary solidity.

'Now, look here,' said Miller, dropping his conciliatory manner very completely, 'you'd better stop this nonsense. I am a police officer, and I am going to come in,' and with this he inserted a massive shoulder and pushed the door open.

'Police officer, are you?' said Ponting. 'And what might your business be with me?'

'That is what I have been waiting to tell you,' said Miller. 'But we don't want to do our talking here.'

'Very well,' growled Ponting. 'Come in. But understand that I am busy. I've been interrupted enough this evening.'

He led the way into a rather barely furnished room with a wide bay-window in which was a table fitted with a writing-slope and lighted by an electric standard lamp. A litter of manuscript explained the nature of his business and his unwillingness to receive casual visitors. He sulkily placed three chairs, and then, seating himself, glowered at Thorndyke and me.

'Are they police officers, too?' he demanded.

'No,' replied Miller, 'they are medical gentlemen. Perhaps you had better explain the matter, doctor,' he added, addressing Thorndyke, who thereupon opened the proceedings.

'We have called,' said he, 'to inform you that Miss Millicent Fawcett died suddenly this evening.'

'The devil!' exclaimed Ponting. 'That's sudden with a vengeance. What time did this happen?'

'About a quarter to nine.'

'Extraordinary!' muttered Ponting. 'I saw her only the day before yesterday, and she seemed quite well then. What did she die of?'

'The appearances,' replied Thorndyke, 'suggest suicide.'

'Suicide!' gasped Ponting. 'Impossible! I can't believe it. Do you mean to tell me she poisoned herself?'

'No,' said Thorndyke, 'it was not poison. Death was caused by injuries to the throat inflicted with a razor.'

'Good God!' exclaimed Ponting. 'What a horrible thing! But,' he added, after a pause, 'I can't believe she did it herself, and I don't. Why should she commit suicide? She was quite happy, and she was just going to be married to that mealy-faced parson. And a razor, too! How do you suppose she came by a razor? Women don't shave. They smoke and drink and swear, but they haven't taken to shaving yet. I don't believe it. Do you?'

He glared ferociously at the superintendent, who replied: 'I am not sure that I do. There's a good deal in what you've just said, and the same objections had occurred to us. But you see, if she didn't do it herself, someone else must have done it, and we should like to find out who that someone is. So we begin by ascertaining where any possible persons may have been at a quarter to nine this evening.'

Ponting smiled like an infuriated cat. 'So you think me a possible person, do you?' said he.

'Everyone is a possible person,' Miller replied blandly, 'especially when he is known to have uttered threats.'

The reply sobered Ponting considerably. For a few moments he sat, looking reflectively at the superintendent; then, in comparatively quiet tones, he said: 'I have been working here since six o'clock. You can see the stuff for yourself, and I can prove that it has been written since six.'

The superintendent nodded, but made no comment, and Ponting gazed at him fixedly, evidently thinking hard. Suddenly he broke into a harsh laugh.

'What is the joke?' Miller inquired stolidly.

'The joke is that I have got another alibi – a very complete one. There are compensations in every evil. I told you I had been interrupted in my work already this evening. It was those fools next door, the Barnetts – cousins of mine.

They are musicians, save the mark! Variety stage, you know. Funny songs and jokes for mental defectives. Well, they practise their infernal ditties in their rooms, and the row comes into mine, and an accursed nuisance it is. However, they have agreed not to practise on Thursdays and Fridays – my busy nights – and usually they don't. But tonight, just as I was in the thick of my writing, I suddenly heard the most unholy din; that idiot, Fred Barnett, bawling one of his imbecile songs – 'When the pigs their wings have folded', and balderdash of that sort – and the other donkey accompanying him on the clarinet, if you please! I stuck it for a minute or two. Then I rushed round to their flat and raised Cain with the bell and knocker. Mrs Fred opened the door, and I told her what I thought of it. Of course she was very apologetic, said they had forgotten that it was Thursday and promised that she would make her husband stop. And I suppose she did, for by the time I got back to my rooms the row had ceased. I could have punched the whole lot of them into a jelly, but it was all for the best as it turns out.'

'What time was it when you went round there?' asked Miller.

'About five minutes past nine,' replied Ponting. 'The church bell had struck nine when the row began.'

'Hm!' grunted Miller, glancing at Thorndyke. 'Well, that is all we wanted to know, so we need not keep you from your work any longer.'

He rose, and being let out with great alacrity, stumped down the stairs, followed by Thorndyke and me. As we came out into the street, he turned to us with a deeply disappointed expression.

'Well,' he exclaimed, 'this is a suck-in. I was in hopes that we had pounced on our quarry before he had got time to clear away the traces. And now we've got it all to do. You can't get round an alibi of that sort.'

I glanced at Thorndyke to see how he was taking this unexpected check. He was evidently puzzled, and I could see by the expression of concentration in his face that he was trying over the facts and inferences in new combinations to meet this new position. Probably he had noticed, as I had, that Ponting was wearing a tweed suit, and that therefore the shreds of clothing from the fence could not be his unless he had changed. But the alibi put him definitely out of the picture, and, as Miller had said, we now had nothing to give us a lead.

Suddenly Thorndyke came out of his reverie and addressed the superintendent.

'We had better put this alibi on the basis of ascertained fact. It ought to be verified at once. At present we have only Ponting's unsupported statement.'

'It isn't likely that he would risk telling a lie,' Miller replied gloomily.

'A man who is under suspicion of murder will risk a good deal,' Thorndyke retorted, 'especially if he is guilty. I think we ought to see Mrs Barnett before there is any opportunity of collusion.'

'There has been time for collusion already,' said Miller. 'Still, you are quite right, and I see there is a light in their sitting room, if that is it, next to Ponting's. Let us go up and settle the matter now. I shall leave you to examine the witness and say what you think it best to say.'

We entered the building and ascended the stairs to the

Barnetts' flat, where Miller rang the bell and executed a double knock. After a short interval the door was opened and a woman looked out at us inquisitively.

'Are you Mrs Frederick Barnett?' Thorndyke inquired. The woman admitted her identity in a tone of some surprise, and Thorndyke explained: 'We have called to make a few inquiries concerning your neighbour, Mr Ponting, and also about certain matters relating to your family. I am afraid it is a rather unseasonable hour for a visit, but as the affair is of some importance and time is an object, I hope you will overlook that.'

Mrs Barnett listened to this explanation with a puzzled and rather suspicious air. After a few moments' hesitation, she said: 'I think you had better see my husband – if you will wait here a moment I will go and tell him.' With this, she pushed the door to, without actually closing it, and we heard her retire along the lobby, presumably to the sitting room. For, during the short colloquy, I had observed a door at the end of the lobby, partly open, through which I could see the end of a table covered with a red cloth.

The 'moment' extended to a full minute, and the superintendent began to show signs of impatience.

'I don't see why you didn't ask her the simple question straight out,' he said, and the same question had occurred to me. But at this point footsteps were heard approaching, the door opened, and a man confronted us, holding the door open with his left hand, his right being wrapped in a handkerchief. He looked suspiciously from one to the other of us, and asked stiffly: 'What is it that you want to know? And would you mind telling me who you are?'

'My name is Thorndyke,' was the reply. 'I am the legal adviser of the Reverend Charles Meade, and these two gentlemen are interested parties. I want to know what you can tell me of Mr Ponting's recent movements – today, for instance. When did you last see him?'

The man appeared to be about to refuse any conversation, but suddenly altered his mind, reflected for a few moments, and then replied: 'I saw him from my window at his – they are bay-windows – about half-past eight. But my wife saw him later than that. If you will come in she can tell you the time exactly.' He led the way along the lobby with an obviously puzzled air. But he was not more puzzled than I, or than Miller, to judge by the bewildered glance that the superintendent cast at me, as he followed our host along the lobby. I was still meditating on Thorndyke's curiously indirect methods when the sitting-room door was opened; and then I got a minor surprise of another kind. When I had last looked into the room, the table had been covered by a red cloth. It was now bare; and when we entered the room I saw that the red cover had been thrown over a side table, on which was some bulky and angular object. Apparently it had been thought desirable to conceal that object, whatever it was, and as we took our seats beside the bare table, my mind was busy with conjectures as to what that object could be.

Mr Barnett repeated Thorndyke's question to his wife, adding: 'I think it must have been a little after nine when Ponting came round. What do you say?'

'Yes,' she replied, 'it would be, for I heard it strike nine just before you began your practice, and he came a few minutes after.'

'You see,' Barnett explained, 'I am a singer, and my brother, here, accompanies me on various instruments, and of course we have to practise. But we don't practise on the nights when Ponting is busy – Thursdays and Fridays – as he said that the music disturbed him. Tonight, however, we made a little mistake. I happen to have got a new song that I am anxious to get ready – it has an illustrative accompaniment on the clarinet, which my brother will play. We were so much taken up with the new song that we all forgot what day of the week it was, and started to have a good practice. But before we had got through the first verse, Ponting came round, battering at the door like a madman. My wife went out and pacified him, and of course we shut down for the evening.'

While Mr Barnett was giving his explanation, I looked about the room with vague curiosity. Somehow – I cannot tell exactly how – I was sensible of something queer in the atmosphere of this place; of a certain indefinite sense of tension. Mrs Barnett looked pale and flurried. Her husband, in spite of his volubility, seemed ill at ease, and the brother, who sat huddled in an easy-chair, nursing a dark-coloured Persian cat, stared into the fire, and neither moved nor spoke. And again I looked at the red tablecloth and wondered what it covered.

'By the way,' said Barnett, after a brief pause, 'what is the point of these inquiries of yours? About Ponting, I mean. What does it matter to you where he was this evening?'

As he spoke, he produced a pipe and tobacco-pouch, and proceeded to fill the former, holding it in his bandaged right hand and filling it with his left. The facility with which he did this suggested that he was left-handed, an inference that was confirmed by the ease with which he struck the match with his left hand, and by the fact that he wore a wristwatch on his right wrist.

'Your question is a perfectly natural one,' said Thorndyke. 'The answer to it is that a very terrible thing has happened. Miss Millicent Fawcett, who is, I think, a connection of yours, met her death this evening under circumstances of grave suspicion. She died, either by her own hand or by the hand of a murderer, a few minutes before nine o'clock. Hence it has become necessary to ascertain the whereabouts at that time of any persons on whom suspicion might reasonably fall.'

'Good God!' exclaimed Barnett. 'What a shocking thing!'

The exclamation was followed by a deep silence, amidst which I could hear the barking of a dog in an adjacent room, the unmistakable sharp, treble yelp of a Pekinese. And again I seemed to be aware of a strange sense of tension in the occupants of this room. On hearing Thorndyke's answer, Mrs Barnett had turned deadly pale and let her head fall forward on her hand. Her husband had sunk onto a chair, and he, too, looked pale and deeply shocked, while the brother continued to stare silently into the fire.

At this moment Thorndyke astonished me by an exhibition of what seemed – under the tragic circumstances – the most outrageous bad manners and bad taste. Rising from his chair with his eyes fixed on a print which hung on the wall above the red-covered table, he said: 'That looks like one of Cameron's etchings,' and forthwith stepped across the room to examine it, resting his hand, as he leaned forward, on the object covered by the cloth.

'Mind where you are putting your hand, sir!' Fred Barnett called out, springing to his feet.

Thorndyke looked down at his hand, and deliberately raising a corner of the cloth, looked under. 'There is no harm done,' he remarked quietly, letting the cloth drop; and with another glance at the print, he went back to his chair.

Once more a deep silence fell upon the room, and I had a vague feeling that the tension had increased. Mrs Barnett was as white as a ghost and seemed to catch at her breath. Her husband watched her with a wild, angry expression and smoked furiously, while the superintendent – also conscious of something abnormal in the atmosphere of the room – looked furtively from the woman to the man and from him to Thorndyke.

Yet again in the silence the shrill barking of the Pekinese dog broke out, and somehow that sound connected itself in my mind with the Persian cat that dozed on the knees of the immovable man by the fire. I looked at the cat and at the man, and even as I looked, I was startled by a most extraordinary apparition. Above the man's shoulder, slowly rose a little round head like the head of a diminutive, greenish-brown man. Higher and higher the tiny monkey raised itself, resting on its little hands to peer at the strangers. Then, with sudden coyness, like a shy baby, it popped down out of sight.

I was thunderstruck. The cat and the dog I had noted merely as a curious coincidence. But the monkey – and such an unusual monkey, too – put coincidences out of the question. I stared at the man in positive stupefaction. Somehow that man was connected with that unforgettable figure lying upon the couch miles away. But how? When that deed of horror was doing, he had been here in this very room. Yet, in some way, he had been concerned in it. And suddenly a suspicion dawned upon me that Thorndyke was waiting for the actual perpetrator to arrive.

'It is a most ghastly affair,' Barnett repeated presently in a husky voice. Then, after a pause, he asked: 'Is there any sort of evidence as to whether she killed herself or was killed by somebody else?'

'I think that my friend, here, Detective Superintendent Miller, has decided that she was murdered.' He looked at the bewildered superintendent, who replied with an inarticulate grunt.

'And is there any clue as to who the – the murderer may be? You spoke of suspected persons just now.'

'Yes,' replied Thorndyke, 'there is an excellent clue, if it can only be followed up. We found a most unmistakable footprint; and what is more, we took a plaster cast of it. Would you like to see the cast?'

Without waiting for a reply, he opened the research-case and took out the cast, which he placed in my hands.

'Just take it round and show it to them,' he said.

The superintendent had witnessed Thorndyke's amazing proceedings with an astonishment that left him speechless. But now he sprang to his feet, and, as I walked round the table, he pressed beside me to guard the precious cast from possible injury. I laid it carefully down on the table, and as the light fell on it obliquely, it presented a most striking appearance – that of a snow-white boot sole on which the unshapely patch, the circular heel, and the marks of wear were clearly visible.

The three spectators gathered round, as near as the superintendent would let them approach, and I observed them closely, assuming that this incomprehensible move of Thorndyke's was a device to catch one or more of them off their guard. Fred Barnett looked at the cast stolidly enough, though his face had gone several shades paler, but Mrs Barnett stared at it with starting eyeballs and dropped jaw – the very picture of horror and dismay. As to James Barnett, whom I now saw clearly for the first time, he stood behind the woman with a singularly scared and haggard face, and his eyes riveted on the white boot sole. And now I could see that he wore a suit of blue serge and that the front both of his coat and waistcoat were thickly covered with the shed hairs of his pets.

There was something very uncanny about this group of persons gathered around that accusing footprint, all as still and rigid as statues and none uttering a sound. But something still more uncanny followed. Suddenly the deep silence of the room was shattered by the shrill notes of a clarinet, and a brassy voice burst forth:

'When the pigs their wings have folded
And the cows are in their nest—'

We all spun round in amazement, and at the first glance the mystery of the crime was solved. There stood Thorndyke with the red table-cover at his feet, and at his side, on the small table, a massively constructed phonograph of the kind used in offices for dictating letters, but fitted with a convoluted metal horn in place of the rubber ear-tubes.

A moment of astonished silence was succeeded by a wild confusion. Mrs Barnett uttered a piercing shriek and fell back onto a chair, her husband broke away and rushed at Thorndyke, who instantly gripped his wrist and pinioned him, while the superintendent, taking in the situation at a glance, fastened on the unresisting James and forced him down into a chair. I ran round, and having stopped the machine – for the preposterous song was hideously incongruous with the tragedy that was enacting – went to Thorndyke's assistance and helped him to remove his prisoner from the neighbourhood of the instrument.

'Superintendent Miller,' said Thorndyke, still maintaining a hold on his squirming captive, 'I believe you are a justice of the peace?'

'Yes,' was the reply, 'ex officio.'

'Then,' said Thorndyke, 'I accuse these three persons of being concerned in the murder of Miss Millicent Fawcett; Frederick Barnett as the principal who actually committed the murder, James Barnett as having aided him by holding the arms of the deceased, and Mrs Barnett as an accessory before the fact in that she worked this phonograph for the purpose of establishing a false alibi.'

'I knew nothing about it!' Mrs Barnett shrieked hysterically. 'They never told me why they wanted me to work the thing.'

'We can't go into that now,' said Miller. 'You will be able to make your defence at the proper time and place. Can one of you go for assistance or must I blow my whistle?'

'You had better go, Jervis,' said Thorndyke. 'I can hold this man until reinforcements arrive. Send a constable up and then go on to the station. And leave the outer door ajar.'

I followed these directions, and having found the police

station, presently returned to the flat with four constables and a sergeant in two taxis.

When the prisoners had been removed, together with the three animals – the latter in charge of a zoophilist constable – we searched the bedrooms. Frederick Barnett had changed his clothing completely, but in a locked drawer – the lock of which Thorndyke picked neatly, to the superintendent's undisguised admiration – we found the discarded garments, including a pair of torn shepherd's plaid trousers, covered with blood stains, and a new, empty razor case. These things, together with the wax cylinder of the phonograph, Miller made up into a neat parcel and took away with him.

'Of course,' said I, as we walked homewards, 'the general drift of this case is quite obvious. But it seemed to me that you went to the Barnetts' flat with a definite purpose already formed, and with a definite suspicion in your mind. Now, I don't see how you came to suspect the Barnetts.'

'I think you will,' he replied, 'if you will recall the incidents in their order from the beginning, including poor Meade's preliminary statement. To begin with the appearances of the body: the suggestion of suicide was transparently false. To say nothing of its incongruity with the character and circumstances of the deceased and the very unlikely weapon used, there were the gashed collar and the cut cap-string. As you know, it is a well-established rule that suicides do not damage their clothing. A man who cuts his own throat doesn't cut his collar. He takes it off. He removes all obstructions. Naturally, for he wishes to complete the act as easily and quickly as possible, and he has time for preparation. But the murderer must take things as he finds them and execute his purpose as best he can.

'But further; the wounds were inflicted near the door, but the body was on the couch at the other end of the room. We saw, from the absence of bleeding, that she was dying – in fact, apparently dead – when she lay down. She must therefore have been carried to the couch after the wounds were inflicted.

'Then there were the bloodstains. They were all in front, and the blood had run down vertically. Then she must have been standing upright while the blood was flowing. Now there were four wounds, and the first one was mortal; it divided the common carotid artery and the great veins. On receiving that wound she would ordinarily have fallen down. But she did not fall, or there would have been a bloodstain across the neck. Why did she not fall? The obvious suggestion was that someone was holding her up. This suggestion was confirmed by the absence of cuts on her hands – which would certainly have been cut if someone had not been holding them. It was further confirmed by the rough crumpling of the collar at the back: so rough that the button was torn off. And we found that button near the door.

'Further, there were the animal hairs. They were on the back only. There were none on the front – where they would have been if derived from the animals – or anywhere else. And we learned that she kept no animals. All these appearances pointed to the presence of two persons, one of whom stood behind her and held her arms while the other stood in front and committed the murder. The cloth on the fence supported this view, being probably derived from two different pairs of trousers. The character of the wounds made it nearly certain that the murderer was left-handed.

'While we were returning in the cab, I reflected on these facts and considered the case generally. First, what was the motive? There was nothing to suggest robbery, nor was it in the least like a robber's crime. What other motive could there be? Well, here was a comparatively rich woman who had made a will in favour of certain persons, and she was going to be married. On her marriage the will would automatically become void, and she was not likely to make another will so favourable to those persons. Here, then, was a possible motive, and that motive applied to Ponting, who had actually uttered threats and was obviously suspect.

'But, apart from those threats, Ponting was not the principal suspect, for he benefited only slightly under the will. The chief beneficiaries were the Barnetts, and Miss Fawcett's death would benefit them, not only by securing the validity of the will, but by setting the will into immediate operation. And there were two of them. They therefore fitted the circumstances better than Ponting did. And when we came to interview Ponting, he went straight out of the picture. His manuscript would probably have cleared him – with his editor's confirmation. But the other alibi was conclusive.

'What instantly struck me, however, was that Ponting's alibi was also an alibi for the Barnetts. But there was this difference: Ponting had been seen; the Barnetts had only been heard. Now, it has often occurred to me that a very effective false alibi could be worked with a gramophone or a phonograph – especially with one on which one can make one's own records. This idea now recurred to me; and at once it was supported by the appearance of an arranged effect. Ponting was known to be at work. It was practically certain that a blast of "music" would bring him out. Then he would be available, if necessary, as a witness to prove an alibi. It seemed to be worthwhile to investigate.

'When we came to the flat we encountered a man with an injured hand – the right. It would have been more striking if it had been his left. But it presently turns out that he is left-handed; which is still more striking as a coincidence. This man is extraordinarily ready to answer questions which most persons would have refused to answer at all. Those answers contain the alibi.

'Then there was the incident of the table – I think you noticed it. That cover was on the large table when we arrived, but it was taken off and thrown over something, evidently to conceal it. But I need not pursue the details. When I had seen the cat, heard the dog, and then seen the monkey, I determined to see what was under the table-cover; and finding that it was a phonograph with the cylinder record still on the drum, I decided to "go Nap" and chance making a mistake. For until we had tried the record, the alibi remained. If it had failed, I should have advised Miller to hold a boot parade. Fortunately we struck the right record and completed the case.'

Mrs Barnett's defence was accepted by the magistrate and the charge against her was dismissed. The other two were committed for trial, and in due course paid the extreme penalty. 'Yet another illustration,' was Thorndyke's comment, 'of the folly of that kind of criminal who won't let well alone, and who will create false clues. If the Barnetts had not laid down those false tracks, they would probably never have been suspected. It was their clever alibi that led us straight to their door.'

Meeting in the Snow

Julian Symons

The snow fell thick and sudden out of a sky that looked like lead. A furious gale sprung from nowhere drove the snowflakes against the windscreen of Francis Quarles's new car. He was gratified to observe that the defroster defrosted, but even so it was not easy to see his way in this world of whirling white. He took a wrong turn, stopped, reversed, and stopped again to look at his map and at his watch. It was now four o'clock and snow had been falling for only an hour, but the road and the surrounding fields were already quite thick.

From the map Quarles saw with relief that he was no more than three miles from Clinton House, where he planned to look in on an old acquaintance named John Landon in the hope of being offered a cup of tea. He had just put the car into gear again when he heard a shout from behind him. A man came running up to the window.

'I say, *do* you think you could give me a lift if you're going anywhere near Clinton House. I've got caught in this *beastly* snow and—' He broke off abruptly and brushed snow from his hair. 'Why, it's Mr Quarles. I'm Geoffrey Landon. You know my Uncle John, and you *have* met me years ago, but I don't suppose you remember.'

'I remember very well.' Geoffrey Landon was the kind of thin spinsterish middle-aged young man who is extremely good at tapestry work, has a nice sense of interior decoration, and is afraid to get his feet wet. As a matter of fact almost the only thing that Quarles remembered about him was that he had quite literally refused to get his feet wet by wading through a shallow pond while out on a walk. He could have hardly been a greater contrast to his uncle, a self-made businessman who was proud of the fact that he still took a cold bath every morning.

John Landon had been a hard man to his children Justin and Eleanor, but Quarles always thought he had showed wonderful toleration in allowing Geoffrey to live with him, and in making him an allowance. Geoffrey was the son of a favourite sister, however, and that perhaps made a difference.

Quarles held the door open. 'I'm passing Clinton House on my way to the coast and I thought of looking in.'

'I'm sure Uncle John will be delighted to see you. I say, what a glamorous car. I really mustn't make it dirty. If you'll excuse me …' Landon opened the boot and put goloshes and stick into it, shook himself in a ladylike manner and slid sinuously into the front seat. As they went slowly along the road he chattered incessantly. Quarles gave three quarters of his attention to driving through the snowstorm, one quarter to what his companion was saying.

'Such weather we have in England, really the south of France is the only place to live. It was quite fine when I walked to Mornley this morning, and not snowing even when I started back after lunch. Then I really got caught in it.'

Quarles put a stop to the flow of chatter by asking after Eleanor and Justin. Eleanor ran the house for her widower father, while Justin had some kind of educational job in Nigeria.

'Eleanor's exactly the same – the eternal spinster, you know. Justin is home now.'

'Finished a tour of duty?' Quarles turned right onto the main road, and saw with relief that the snow was now beating against the side windows instead of the front.

'Yes. But he's not going back to Nigeria. Getting married instead, and settling down to look after the estate. Justin wanted to start up on his own as a farmer, but the old man wouldn't put up the money. I'm going up to London to live – Justin will be home now, and we never *did* get on.'

Going up to be an interior decorator, Quarles thought. As if in answer to these unspoken words Geoffrey prattled: 'Adrian Hastings, that's a friend of mine, is doing simply terribly well with a thing he's started called Artistic Interiors – he advises on interior decoration you know. And I'm going in with him. I really have rather a flair for matching colours.'

'I'm sure you have. Is Eleanor staying at home?'

'Yes. She wanted to start her own dressmaking business not long ago, but there again Uncle John wouldn't put up the money. Wanted to keep his housekeeper, I expect – and he was very wise, too. She really has no dress sense. Here we are.'

Clinton House stood by itself, with uninterrupted views over open country. They stepped out into whirling snow and Geoffrey led the way into the porch. 'Justin's gone up to London to see his dear Helen. He's very much struck, I assure you. And it's cook's afternoon off and I think Eleanor may have gone in to Shepston to do some shopping. But Uncle John's certainly at home, and I'll make us all a nice cup of tea.'

He opened the front door and called, but there was no answer. 'I expect he's having a snooze in the library. I'll just go through and see.' They went down a passage, turned to the right, and Geoffrey opened a door. Then he put his hand to his mouth and cried out.

Standing behind him, Quarles could see the body of John Landon on the floor. There was a neat hole, hardly more than a puncture, where a bullet had gone through his forehead.

Some time later Quarles was talking to three very subdued people in the drawing room. The doctor had been and gone, confirming the obvious fact that John Landon had been killed by a shot through the forehead at close range. He had been shot with his own revolver, which lay near him on the floor. The murderer had come in through the French windows of the library, shot John Landon, and apparently gone out again the same way. There were scuffed-up footprints on the terrace outside the door, now half-covered by snow. They led a few yards into a small wood at the back of the house, and there were lost. The murder had taken place between three o'clock and half past.

'You must face the fact that you are all suspects,' Quarles

said. 'And that you all had motives of a sort. Justin, you wanted to start your own farm and your father insisted that you look after the estate. Eleanor, he refused you the money to start a dressmaking business. Geoffrey, you were being pushed out of your home because Justin was coming to live in it.'

'Uncle was giving me money to go into business,' Geoffrey said.

Eleanor, thin, pale and intense, caught him up. 'But he was stopping your allowance. For good. As for me, it's absurd to think that I'd kill him because he refused me a little money.'

Justin, rosy-faced and rugged, spoke. 'Or that I would because of our differences about the farm. I admit I was angry, but that's a very different thing from ...' His voice trailed off.

'Then I understand that you all knew the terms of his will. Geoffrey, you get ten thousand pounds, Eleanor gets twenty-five thousand. Justin gets the rest of the estate which must mean that he's now quite a rich man. So much for motive. What about opportunity? Where were you between three o'clock and half past, Geoffrey?'

'I was walking back from Mornley. It's nearly ten miles from Clinton House, and I started back just after two o'clock. I'd done almost seven miles when I met you at four.

'Justin?'

'I was in the train coming back from London. And I'll save you the trouble of asking questions by saying that nobody saw me off at the London end, and that the ticket collector didn't seem to be on duty when I arrived here, so I just walked out.'

'You can't prove that you didn't come back on an earlier train?'

'No, I don't suppose I can.'

'Eleanor?'

'I took the bus in to Shepston – it's just under three miles. Then I missed the three-fifteen bus back, so I decided to walk rather than wait an hour and a half for the next bus.'

'You decided to walk – in that snow?'

She shrugged her shoulders. 'I don't mind a little snow. And it wasn't snowing very hard then.'

'You didn't pass anyone on your way home?'

'No, I don't think I did.'

'One good alibi – and two that are hardly alibis at all.' Quarles looked at Geoffrey Landon. 'And the murderer has the good alibi.'

They goggled at him. Then Geoffrey Landon said in an outraged voice: 'You can't mean me. I couldn't possibly have done it. You picked me up yourself.'

'Has Geoffrey got a bicycle or a motorbike?' Quarles asked Eleanor.

'A bicycle.'

'Very well. Your alibi was simply made, Geoffrey. You left your bicycle hidden in some convenient spot outside Mornley, stayed there until two o'clock, rode back on the bicycle which you left in the wood, shot your uncle, and rode off again. You then parked the bicycle in a disused shepherd's hut or some other convenient place – I should imagine very near where you met me – and set out on foot to find a passing motorist to verify your alibi. You were unlucky to find me.'

'If you look for yourself, Mr Clever Quarles,' Geoffrey said, 'you'll find my bicycle in the shed outside.'

Quarles nodded indulgently. 'Then you bought another one. But we shall find it, don't worry, and trace it to you.'

Justin Landon spoke hesitantly. 'All this is the purest conjecture.'

'Oh no. You see, Geoffrey doesn't like to get his feet wet. That's the only thing I remembered about him. Sure enough, when I picked him up he was wearing goloshes.'

Geoffrey Landon gave a gasp of pure terror. Eleanor, puzzled, said: 'What about it? It was snowing?'

'Don't you see? Geoffrey went in to Mornley this morning when it was quite fine. He told me himself that it wasn't snowing when he started back, so he couldn't have been wearing them then. So that the only place he could have got them is back at the house here, where he put them on before going out into the snow again after killing his uncle. A man prepared to commit murder,' Quarles said thoughtfully, 'really shouldn't be afraid of getting his feet wet.'

The Chopham Affair

Edgar Wallace

Lawyers who write books are not, as a rule, popular with their confrères, but Archibald Lenton, the most brilliant of prosecuting attorneys, was an exception. He kept a case-book and published extracts from time to time. He has not published his theories on the Chopham affair, though I believe he formulated one. I present him with the facts of the case and the truth about Alphonse or Alphonso Riebiera.

This was a man who had a way with women, especially women who had not graduated in the more worldly school of experience. He described himself as a Spaniard, though his passport was issued by a South American republic. Sometimes he presented visiting cards which were inscribed 'Le Marquis de Riebiera', but that was only on very special occasions.

He was young, with an olive complexion, faultless features, and showed his two rows of dazzling white teeth when he smiled. He found it convenient to change his appearance. For example: when he was a hired dancer attached to the personnel of an Egyptian hotel he wore little side whiskers which, oddly enough, exaggerated his youthfulness; in the casino at Enghien, where by some means he secured the position of croupier, he was decorated with a little black moustache. Staid, sober and unimaginative spectators of his many adventures were irritably amazed that women said anything to him, but then it is notoriously difficult for any man, even an unimaginative man, to discover attractive qualities in successful lovers.

And yet the most unlikely women came under his spell and had to regret it. There arrived a time when he became a patron of the gambling establishments where he had been the most humble and the least trusted of servants, when he lived royally in hotels where he once was hired at so many piastre per dance. Diamonds came to his spotless shirt-front, pretty manicurists tended his nails and received fees larger than his one-time dancing partners had slipped shyly into his hand.

There were certain gross men who played interminable dominoes in the cheaper cafés that abound on the unfashionable side of the Seine, who are amazing news centres. They know how the oddest people live, and they were very plain-spoken when they discussed Alphonse. They could tell you, though Heaven knows how the information came to them, of fat registered letters that came to him in his flat in the Boulevard Haussmann. Registered letters stuffed with money, and despairing letters that said in effect (and in various languages): 'I can send you no more – this is the last.' But they did send more.

Alphonse had developed a well-organised business. He would leave for London, or Rome, or Amsterdam, or Vienna, or even Athens, arriving at his destination by sleeping-car, drive to the best hotel, hire a luxurious suite – and telephone. Usually the unhappy lady met him by appointment, tearful, hysterically furious, bitter, insulting, but always remunerative.

For when Alphonse read extracts from the letters they had sent to him in the day of the Great Glamour and told them what their husbands' income was almost to a pound, lira, franc or guilder, they reconsidered their decision to tell their husbands everything, and Alphonse went back to Paris with his allowance.

This was his method with the bigger game; sometimes he announced his coming visit with a letter discreetly worded, which made personal application unnecessary. He was not very much afraid of husbands or brothers; the philosophy which had germinated from his experience made him contemptuous of human nature. He believed that most people were cowards and lived in fear of their lives, and greater fear of their regulations. He carried two silver-plated revolvers, one in each hip-pocket. They had prettily damascened barrels and ivory handles carved in the likeness of nymphs. He bought them in Cairo from a man who smuggled cocaine from Vienna.

Alphonse had some twenty 'clients' on his books, and added to them as opportunity arose. Of the twenty, five were gold mines (he thought of them as such), the remainder were silver mines.

There was a silver mine living in England, a very lovely,

rather sad-looking girl, who was happily married, except when she thought of Alphonse. She loved her husband and hated herself and hated Alphonse intensely and impotently. Having a fortune of her own she could pay – therefore she paid.

Then in a fit of desperate revolt she wrote saying: 'This is the last, etc.' Alphonse was amused. He waited until September when the next allowance was due, and it did not come. Nor in October, nor November. In December he wrote to her; he did not wish to go to England in December, for England is very gloomy and foggy, and it was so much nicer in Egypt; but business was business.

His letter reached its address when the woman to whom it was addressed was on a visit to her aunt in Long Island. She had been born an American. Alphonse had not written in answer to her letter; she had sailed for New York feeling safe.

Her husband, whose initial was the same as his wife's, opened the letter by accident and read it through very carefully. He was no fool. He did not regard the wife he wooed as an outcast; what happened before his marriage was her business – what happened now was his.

And he understood these wild dreams of her, and her wild, uncontrollable weeping for no reason at all, and he knew what the future held for her.

He went to Paris and made enquiries: he sought the company of the gross men who play dominoes, and heard much that was interesting.

Alphonse arrived in London and telephoned from a call-box. Madam was not at home. A typewritten letter came to him, making an appointment for the Wednesday. It was the usual rendezvous, the hour specified, an injunction to secrecy. The affair ran normally.

He passed his time pleasantly in the days of waiting. Bought a new Spanza car of the latest model, arranged for its transportation to Paris and, in the meantime, amused himself by driving it.

At the appointed hour he arrived, knocked at the door of the house and was admitted …

Riebiera, green of face, shaking at the knees, surrendered his two ornamented pistols without a fight …

At eight o'clock on Christmas morning Superintendent Oakington was called from his warm bed by telephone and was told the news.

A milkman driving across Chopham Common had seen a car standing a little off the road. It was apparently a new car, and must have been standing in its position all night. There were three inches of snow on its roof, beneath the body of the car the bracken was green.

An arresting sight even for a milkman who, at seven o'clock on a wintry morning, had no other thought than to supply the needs of his customers as quickly as possible and return at the earliest moment to his own home and the festivities and feastings proper to the day.

He got out of the Ford he was driving and stamped through the snow. He saw a man lying face downwards, and in his grey hand a silver-barrelled revolver. He was dead. And then the startled milkman saw the second man. His face was invisible: it lay under a thick mask of snow that made his pinched features grotesque and hideous.

The milkman ran back to his car and drove towards a police station.

Mr Oakington was on the spot within an hour of being called. There were a dozen policemen grouped around the car and the shapes in the snow; the reporters, thank God, had not arrived.

Late in the afternoon the superintendent put a call through to one man who might help in a moment of profound bewilderment.

Archibald Lenton was the most promising of Treasury Juniors that the Bar had known for years. The Common Law Bar lifts its delicate nose at lawyers who are interested in criminal cases to the exclusion of other practice. But Archie Lenton survived the unspoken disapproval of his brethren and, concentrating on this unsavoury aspect of jurisprudence, was both a successful advocate and an authority on certain types of crime, for he had written a textbook which was accepted as authoritative.

An hour later he was in the superintendent's room at Scotland Yard, listening to the story.

'We've identified both men. One is a foreigner, a man from the Argentine, so far as I can discover from his passport, named Alphonse or Alphonso Riebiera. He lives in Paris, and has been in this country for about a week.'

'Well off?'

'Very, I should say. We found about two hundred pounds in his pocket. He was staying at the Nederland Hotel, and bought a car for twelve hundred pounds only last Friday, paying cash. That is the car we found near the body. I've been on the 'phone to Paris, and he is suspected there of being a blackmailer. The police have searched and sealed his flat, but found no documents of any kind. He is evidently the sort of man who keeps his business under his hat.'

'He was shot, you say? How many times?'

'Once, through the head. The other man was killed in exactly the same way. There was a trace of blood in the car, but nothing else.'

Mr Lenton jotted down a note on a pad of paper.

'Who was the other man?' he asked.

'That's the queerest thing of all – an old acquaintance of yours.'

'Mine? Who on earth—?'

'Do you remember a fellow you defended on a murder charge – Joe Stackett?'

'At Exeter, good lord, yes! Was that the man?'

'We've identified him from his fingerprints. As a matter of fact, we were after Joe – he's an expert car thief who only came out of prison last week; he got away with a car yesterday morning, but abandoned it after a chase and slipped through the fingers of the Flying Squad. Last night he pinched an old car from a second-hand dealer and was spotted and chased. We found the car abandoned in Tooting. He was never seen again until he was picked up on the Chopham Common.'

Archie Lenton leant back in his chair and stared thoughtfully at the ceiling.

'He stole the Spanza – the owner jumped on the running-board and there was a fight—' he began, but the superintendent shook his head.

'Where did he get his gun? English criminals do not carry guns. And they weren't ordinary revolvers. Silver-plated, ivory butts carved with girls' figures – both identical. There were fifty pounds in Joe's pocket; they are consecutive numbers to those found in Riebiera's pocket-book. If he'd stolen them he'd have taken the lot. Joe wouldn't stop at murder, you know that, Mr Lenton. He killed that old woman in Exeter, although he was acquitted. Riebiera must have given him the fifty—'

A telephone bell rang; the superintendent drew the instrument towards him and listened. After ten minutes of a conversation which was confined, so far as Oakington was concerned, to a dozen brief questions, he put down the receiver.

'One of my officers has traced the movements of the car; it was seen standing outside "Greenlawns", a house in Tooting. It was there at nine forty-five and was seen by a postman. If you feel like spending Christmas night doing a little bit of detective work, we'll go down and see the place.'

They arrived half an hour later at a house in a very respectable neighbourhood. The two detectives who waited their coming had obtained the keys, but had not gone inside. The house was for sale and was standing empty. It was the property of two old maiden ladies who had placed the premises in an agent's hands when they had moved into the country.

The appearance of the car before an empty house had aroused the interest of the postman. He had seen no lights in the windows, and decided that the machine was owned by one of the guests at the next-door house.

Oakington opened the door and switched on the light. Strangely enough, the old ladies had not had the current disconnected, though they were notoriously mean. The passage was bare, except for a pair of bead curtains which hung from an arched support to the ceiling.

The front room drew blank. It was in one of the back rooms on the ground floor that they found evidence of the crime. There was blood on the bare planks of the floor and in the grate a litter of ashes.

'Somebody has burnt paper – I smelt it when I came into the room,' said Lenton.

He knelt before the grate and lifted a handful of fine ashes carefully.

'And these have been stirred up until there isn't an ash big enough to hold a word,' he said.

He examined the blood-prints and made a careful scrutiny of the walls. The window was covered with a shutter.

'That kept the light from getting in,' he said, 'and the sound of the shot getting out. There is nothing else here.'

The detective-sergeant who was inspecting the other rooms returned with the news that a kitchen window had been forced. There was one muddy print on the kitchen table which was under the window, and a rough attempt had been made to obliterate this. Behind the house was a large garden and behind that an allotment. It would be easy to reach and enter the house without exciting attention.

'But if Stackett was being chased by the police why should he come here?' he asked.

'His car was found abandoned not more than two hundred yards from here,' explained Oakington. 'He may have entered the house in the hope of finding something valuable, and have been surprised by Riebiera.'

Archie Lenton laughed softly.

'I can give you a better theory than that,' he said, and for the greater part of the night he wrote carefully and convincingly, reconstructing the crime, giving the most minute details.

That account is still preserved at Scotland Yard, and there are many highly placed officials who swear by it.

And yet something altogether different happened on the night of that 24th of December …

The streets were greasy, the car-lines abominably so. Stackett's mean little car slithered and skidded alarmingly. He had been in a bad temper when he started out on his hungry quest; he grew sour and savage with the evening passing on with nothing to show for his discomfort.

The suburban high street was crowded too; street cars moved at a crawl, their bells clanging pathetically; street vendors had their stalls jammed end to end on either side of the thoroughfare; stalls green and red with holly wreaths and untidy bunches of mistletoe; there were butcher stalls, raucous auctioneers holding masses of raw beef and roaring their offers; vegetable stalls; stalls piled high with plates and cups and saucers and gaudy dishes and glassware, shining in the rays of the powerful acetylene lamps …

The car skidded. There was a crash and a scream. Breaking crockery has an alarming sound … A yell from the stall owner; Stackett straightened his machine and darted between a tramcar and a trolley …

'Hi, you!'

He twisted his wheel, almost knocked down the policeman who came to intercept him, and swung into a dark side street, his foot clamped on the accelerator. He turned to the right and the left, to the right again. Here was a long suburban road; houses monotonously alike on either side, terribly dreary brick blocks where men and women and children lived, were born, paid rent, and died. A mile further on he passed the gateway of the cemetery where they found the rest which was their supreme reward for living at all.

The police whistle had followed him for less than a quarter of a mile. He had passed a policeman running towards the sound – anyway, flatties never worried Stackett. Some of his ill humour passed in the amusement which the sight of the running copper brought.

Bringing the noisy little car to a standstill by the side of the road, he got down, and, relighting the cigarette he had so carefully extinguished, he gazed glumly at the stained and battered mudguard which was shivering and shaking under the pulsations of the engine …

Through that same greasy street came a motorcyclist, muffled to the chin, his goggles dangling about his neck. He pulled up his shining wheel near the policeman on point duty and, supporting his balance with one foot in the muddy road, asked questions.

'Yes, sergeant,' said the policeman. 'I saw him. He went down there. As a matter of fact, I was going to pinch him for driving to the common danger, but he hopped it.'

'That's Joe Stackett,' nodded Sergeant Kenton of the CID. 'A thin-faced man with a pointed nose?'

The point-duty policeman had not seen the face behind the windscreen, but he had seen the car, and that he described accurately.

'Stolen from Elmer's garage. At least, Elmer will say so, but he probably provided it. Dumped stuff. Which way did you say?'

The policeman indicated, and the sergeant kicked his engine to life and went chug-chugging down the dark street.

He missed Mr Stackett by a piece of bad luck – bad luck for everybody, including Mr Stackett, who was at the beginning of his amazing adventure.

Switching off the engine, he had continued on foot. About fifty yards away was the wide opening of a road superior in class to any he had traversed. Even the dreariest suburb has its West End, and here were villas standing on their own acres – very sedate villas, with porches and porch lamps in wrought-iron and oddly coloured glass, and shaven lawns, and rose gardens swathed in matting, and no two villas were alike. At the far end he saw a red light, and his heart leapt with joy. Christmas – it was to be Christmas after all, with good food and lashings of drink and other manifestations of happiness and comfort peculiarly attractive to Joe Stackett.

It looked like a car worth knocking off, even in the darkness. He saw somebody near the machine and stopped. It was difficult to tell in the gloom whether the person near the car had got in or had come out. He listened. There came to him neither the slam of the driver's door nor the whine of the self-starter. He came a little closer, walked boldly on, his restless eyes moving left and right for danger. All the houses were occupied. Bright lights illuminated the casement cloth which covered the windows. He heard the sound of revelry and two gramophones playing dance tunes. But his eyes always came back to the polished limousine at the door of the end house. There was no light there. It was completely dark, from the gabled attic to the ground floor.

He quickened his pace. It was a Spanza. His heart leapt at the recognition. For a Spanza is a car for which there is a ready sale. You can get as much as a hundred pounds for a new one. They are popular amongst Eurasians and wealthy Hindus. Binky Jones, who was the best car fence in London, would pay him cash, not less than sixty. In a week's time that car would be crated and on its way to India, there to be resold at a handsome profit.

The driver's door was wide open. He heard the soft purr of the engine. He slid into the driver's seat, closed the door noiselessly, and almost without as much as a whine the Spanza moved on.

It was a new one, brand new ... A hundred at least.

Gathering speed, he passed to the end of the road, came to a wide common and skirted it. Presently he was in another shopping street, but he knew too much to turn back towards London. He would take the open country for it, work round through Esher and come into London by the Portsmouth Road. The art of car-stealing is to move as quickly as possible from the police division where the machine is stolen and may be instantly reported, to a 'foreign' division which will not know of the theft until hours after.

There might be all sorts of extra pickings. There was a big luggage trunk behind and possibly a few knick-knacks in the body of the car itself. At a suitable moment he would make a leisurely search. At the moment he headed for Epsom, turning back to hit the Kingston bypass. Sleet fell – snow and rain together. He set the screen-wiper working and began to hum a little tune. The Kingston bypass was deserted. It was too unpleasant a night for much traffic.

Mr Stackett was debating what would be the best place to make his search when he felt an unpleasant draught behind him. He had noticed there was a sliding window separating the interior of the car from the driver's seat, which had possibly worked loose. He put up his hand to push it close.

'Drive on, don't turn round or I'll blow your head off.'

Involuntarily he half turned to see the gaping muzzle of an automatic, and in his agitation put his foot on the brake. The car skidded from one side of the road to the other, half turned and recovered.

'Drive on, I am telling you,' said a metallic voice. 'When you reach the Portsmouth Road turn and bear towards Weybridge. If you attempt to stop I will shoot you. Is that clear?'

Joe Stackett's teeth were chattering. He could not articulate the 'yes'. All that he could do was to nod. He went on nodding for half a mile before he realised what he was doing.

No further word came from the interior of the car until they passed the racecourse; then unexpectedly the voice gave a new direction:

'Turn left towards Leatherhead.'

The driver obeyed.

They came to a stretch of common. Stackett, who knew the country well, realised the complete isolation of the spot.

'Slow down, pull in to the left ... There is no dip there. You can switch on your lights.'

The car slid and bumped over the uneven ground, the wheels crunched through beds of bracken ...

'Stop.'

The door behind him opened. The man got out. He jerked open the driver's door.

'Step down,' he said. 'Turn out your lights first. Have you got a gun?'

'Gun? Why the hell should I have a gun?' stammered the car thief.

He was focused all the time in a ring of light from a very bright electric torch which the passenger had turned upon him.

'You are an act of Providence.'

Stackett could not see the face of the speaker. He saw only the gun in the hand, for the stranger kept this well in the light.

'Look inside the car.'

Stackett looked and almost collapsed. There was a figure huddled in one corner of the seat – the figure of a man. He saw something else – a bicycle jammed into the car, one wheel touching the roof, the other on the floor. He saw the man's white face … Dead! A slim, rather short man, with dark hair and a dark moustache, a foreigner. There was a little red hole in his temple.

'Pull him out,' commanded the voice sharply.

Stackett shrank back, but a powerful hand pushed him towards the car.

'Pull him out!'

With his face moist with cold perspiration, the car thief obeyed; put his hands under the armpits of the inanimate figure, dragged him out and laid him on the bracken.

'He's dead,' he whimpered.

'Completely,' said the other.

Suddenly he switched off his electric torch. Far away came a gleam of light on the road, corning swiftly towards them. It was a car moving towards Esher. It passed.

'I saw you coming just after I had got the body into the car. There wasn't time to get back to the house. I'd hoped you were just an ordinary pedestrian. When I saw you get into the car I guessed pretty well your vocation. What is your name?'

'Joseph Stackett.'

'Stackett?'

The light flashed on his face again. 'How wonderful! Do you remember the Exeter Assizes? The old woman you killed with a hammer? I defended you!'

Joe's eyes were wide open. He stared past the light at the dim grey thing that was a face.

'Mr Lenton?' he said hoarsely. 'Good God, sir!'

'You murdered her in cold blood for a few paltry shillings, and you would have been dead now, Stackett, if I hadn't found a flaw in the evidence. You expected to die, didn't you? You remember how we used to talk in Exeter Gaol about the trap that would not work when they tried to hang a murderer, and the ghoulish satisfaction you had that you would stand on the same trap?'

Joe Stackett grinned uncomfortably.

'And I meant it, sir,' he said, 'but you can't try a man twice—'

Then his eyes dropped to the figure at his feet, the dapper little man with a black moustache, with a red hole in his temple.

Lenton leant over the dead man, took out a pocket case

from the inside of the jacket and at his leisure detached ten notes.

'Put these in your pocket.'

He obeyed, wondering what service would be required of him, wondered more why the pocket-book with its precious notes was returned to the dead man's pocket.

Lenton looked back along the road. Snow was falling now, real snow. It came down in small particles, falling so thickly that it seemed that a fog lay on the land.

'You fit into this perfectly … a man unfit to live. There is fate in this meeting.'

'I don't know what you mean by fate.'

Joe Stackett grew bold: he had to deal with a lawyer and a gentleman who, in a criminal sense, was his inferior. The money obviously had been given to him to keep his mouth shut.

'What have you been doing, Mr Lenton? That's bad, ain't it? This fellow's dead and—'

He must have seen the pencil of flame that came from the other's hand. He could have felt nothing, for he was dead before he sprawled over the body on the ground.

Mr Archibald Lenton examined the revolver by the light of his lamp, opened the breech and closed it again. Stooping, he laid it near the hand of the little man with the black moustache and, lifting the body of Joe Stackett, he dragged it towards the car and let it drop. Bending down, he clasped the still warm hands about the butt of another pistol. Then, at his leisure, he took the bicycle from the interior of the car and carried it back to the road. It was already white and fine snow was falling in sheets.

Mr Lenton went on and reached his home two hours later, when the bells of the local Anglo-Catholic church were ringing musically.

There was a cable waiting for him from his wife:

A Happy Christmas to you, darling.

He was ridiculously pleased that she had remembered to send the wire – he was very fond of his wife.

The Adventure of the Abbey Grange

Arthur Conan Doyle

It was on a bitterly cold and frosty morning, towards the end of the winter of '97, that I was awakened by a tugging at my shoulder. It was Holmes. The candle in his hand shone upon his eager, stooping face, and told me at a glance that something was amiss.

'Come, Watson, come!' he cried. 'The game is afoot. Not a word! Into your clothes and come!'

Ten minutes later we were both in a cab, and rattling through the silent streets on our way to Charing Cross Station. The first faint winter's dawn was beginning to appear, and we could dimly see the occasional figure of an early workman as he passed us, blurred and indistinct in the opalescent London reek. Holmes nestled in silence into his heavy coat, and I was glad to do the same, for the air was most bitter, and neither of us had broken our fast.

It was not until we had consumed some hot tea at the station and taken our places in the Kentish train that we were sufficiently thawed, he to speak and I to listen. Holmes drew a note from his pocket, and read aloud:

Abbey Grange, Marsham, Kent, 3:30 AM

MY DEAR MR HOLMES:

I should be very glad of your immediate assistance in what promises to be a most remarkable case. It is something quite in your line. Except for releasing the lady I will see that everything is kept exactly as I have found it, but I beg you not to lose an instant, as it is difficult to leave Sir Eustace there.

Yours faithfully,

STANLEY HOPKINS

'Hopkins has called me in seven times, and on each occasion his summons has been entirely justified,' said Holmes. 'I fancy that every one of his cases has found its way into your collection, and I must admit, Watson, that you have some power of selection, which atones for much which I deplore in your narratives. Your fatal habit of looking at everything from the point of view of a story instead of as a scientific exercise has ruined what might have been an instructive and even classical series of demonstrations. You slur over work of the utmost finesse and delicacy, in order to dwell upon sensational details which may excite, but cannot possibly instruct, the reader.'

'Why do you not write them yourself?' I said, with some bitterness.

'I will, my dear Watson, I will. At present I am, as you know, fairly busy, but I propose to devote my declining years to the composition of a textbook, which shall focus the whole art of detection into one volume. Our present research appears to be a case of murder.'

'You think this Sir Eustace is dead, then?'

'I should say so. Hopkins's writing shows considerable agitation, and he is not an emotional man. Yes, I gather there has been violence, and that the body is left for our inspection. A mere suicide would not have caused him to send for me. As to the release of the lady, it would appear that she has been locked in her room during the tragedy. We are moving in high life, Watson, crackling paper, "E. B." monogram, coat-of-arms, picturesque address. I think that friend Hopkins will live up to his reputation, and that we shall have an interesting morning. The crime was committed before twelve last night.'

'How can you possibly tell?'

'By an inspection of the trains, and by reckoning the time. The local police had to be called in, they had to communicate with Scotland Yard, Hopkins had to go out, and he in turn had to send for me. All that makes a fair night's work. Well, here we are at Chislehurst Station, and we shall soon set our doubts at rest.'

A drive of a couple of miles through narrow country lanes brought us to a park gate, which was opened for us by an old lodge-keeper, whose haggard face bore the reflection of some great disaster. The avenue ran through a noble park, between lines of ancient elms, and ended in a low, wide-spread house, pillared in front after the fashion of Palladio. The central part was evidently of a great age and shrouded in ivy, but the large windows showed that modern changes had been carried out, and one wing of the house appeared to be entirely new. The youthful figure and alert, eager face of Inspector Stanley Hopkins confronted us in the open doorway.

'I'm very glad you have come, Mr Holmes. And you, too, Dr Watson. But, indeed, if I had my time over again, I should not have troubled you, for since the lady has come to herself, she has given so clear an account of the affair that there is not much left for us to do. You remember that Lewisham gang of burglars?'

'What, the three Randalls?'

'Exactly; the father and two sons. It's their work. I have not a doubt of it. They did a job at Sydenham a fortnight ago and were seen and described. Rather cool to do another so soon and so near, but it is they, beyond all doubt. It's a hanging matter this time.'

'Sir Eustace is dead, then?'

'Yes, his head was knocked in with his own poker.'

'Sir Eustace Brackenstall, the driver tells me.'

'Exactly – one of the richest men in Kent – Lady Brackenstall is in the morning room. Poor lady, she has had a most dreadful experience. She seemed half dead when I saw her first. I think you had best see her and hear her account of the facts. Then we will examine the dining room together.'

Lady Brackenstall was no ordinary person. Seldom have I seen so graceful a figure, so womanly a presence, and so beautiful a face. She was a blonde, golden-haired, blue-eyed, and would no doubt have had the perfect complexion which goes with such colouring, had not her recent experience left her drawn and haggard. Her sufferings were physical as well as mental, for over one eye rose a hideous, plum-coloured swelling, which her maid, a tall, austere woman, was bathing assiduously with vinegar and water. The lady lay back exhausted upon a couch, but her quick, observant gaze, as we entered the room, and the alert expression of her beautiful features, showed that neither her wits nor her courage had been shaken by her terrible experience. She was enveloped in a loose dressing gown of blue and silver, but a black sequin-covered dinner dress lay upon the couch beside her.

'I have told you all that happened, Mr Hopkins,' she said, wearily. 'Could you not repeat it for me? Well, if you think it necessary, I will tell these gentlemen what occurred. Have they been in the dining room yet?'

'I thought they had better hear your ladyship's story first.'

'I shall be glad when you can arrange matters. It is horrible to me to think of him still lying there.' She shuddered and buried her face in her hands. As she did so, the loose gown fell back from her forearms. Holmes uttered an exclamation.

'You have other injuries, madam! What is this?' Two vivid red spots stood out on one of the white, round limbs. She hastily covered it.

'It is nothing. It has no connection with this hideous business tonight. If you and your friend will sit down, I will tell you all I can.

'I am the wife of Sir Eustace Brackenstall. I have been married about a year. I suppose that it is no use my attempting to conceal that our marriage has not been a happy one. I fear that all our neighbours would tell you that, even if I were to attempt to deny it. Perhaps the fault may be partly mine. I was brought up in the freer, less conventional atmosphere of South Australia, and this English life, with its proprieties and its primness, is not congenial to me. But the main reason lies in the one fact, which is notorious to everyone, and that is that Sir Eustace was a confirmed drunkard. To be with such a man for an hour is unpleasant. Can you imagine what it means for a sensitive and high-spirited woman to be tied to him for day and night? It is a sacrilege, a crime, a villainy to hold that such a marriage is binding. I say that these monstrous laws of yours will bring a curse upon the land – God will not let such wickedness endure.' For an instant she sat up, her cheeks flushed, and her eyes blazing from under the terrible mark upon her brow. Then the strong, soothing hand of the austere maid drew her head down on to the cushion, and the wild anger died away into passionate sobbing. At last she continued:

'I will tell you about last night. You are aware, perhaps, that in this house all the servants sleep in the modern wing. This central block is made up of the dwelling rooms, with the kitchen behind and our bedroom above. My maid, Theresa, sleeps above my room. There is no one else, and no sound could alarm those who are in the farther wing. This must have been well-known to the robbers, or they would not have acted as they did.

'Sir Eustace retired about half-past ten. The servants had

already gone to their quarters. Only my maid was up, and she had remained in her room at the top of the house until I needed her services. I sat until after eleven in this room, absorbed in a book. Then I walked round to see that all was right before I went upstairs. It was my custom to do this myself, for, as I have explained, Sir Eustace was not always to be trusted. I went into the kitchen, the butler's pantry, the gun room, the billiard room, the drawing room, and finally the dining room. As I approached the window, which is covered with thick curtains, I suddenly felt the wind blow upon my face and realised that it was open. I flung the curtain aside and found myself face to face with a broad-shouldered elderly man, who had just stepped into the room. The window is a long French one, which really forms a door leading to the lawn. I held my bedroom candle lit in my hand, and, by its light, behind the first man I saw two others, who were in the act of entering. I stepped back, but the fellow was on me in an instant. He caught me first by the wrist and then by the throat. I opened my mouth to scream, but he struck me a savage blow with his fist over the eye, and felled me to the ground. I must have been unconscious for a few minutes, for when I came to myself, I found that they had torn down the bell-rope, and had secured me tightly to the oaken chair which stands at the head of the dining table. I was so firmly bound that I could not move, and a handkerchief round my mouth prevented me from uttering a sound. It was at this instant that my unfortunate husband entered the room. He had evidently heard some suspicious sounds, and he came prepared for such a scene as he found. He was dressed in nightshirt and trousers, with his favourite blackthorn cudgel in his hand. He rushed at the burglars, but another – it was an elderly man – stooped, picked the poker out of the grate and struck him a horrible blow as he passed. He fell with a groan and never moved again. I fainted once more, but again it could only have been for a very few minutes during which I was insensible. When I opened my eyes I found that they had collected the silver from the sideboard, and they had drawn a bottle of wine which stood there. Each of them had a glass in his hand. I have already told you, have I not, that one was elderly, with a beard, and the others young, hairless lads. They might have been a father with his two sons. They talked together in whispers. Then they came over and made sure that I was securely bound. Finally they withdrew, closing the window after them. It was quite a quarter of an hour before I got my mouth free. When I did so, my screams brought the maid to my assistance. The other servants were soon alarmed, and we sent for the local police, who instantly communicated with London. That is really all that I can tell you, gentlemen, and I trust that it will not be necessary for me to go over so painful a story again.'

'Any questions, Mr Holmes?' asked Hopkins.

'I will not impose any further tax upon Lady Brackenstall's patience and time,' said Holmes. 'Before I go into the dining room, I should like to hear your experience.' He looked at the maid.

'I saw the men before ever they came into the house,' said she. 'As I sat by my bedroom window I saw three men in the moonlight down by the lodge gate yonder, but I thought nothing of it at the time. It was more than an hour after that I heard my mistress scream, and down I ran, to find her, poor lamb, just as she says, and him on the floor, with his blood and brains over the room. It was enough to drive a woman out of her wits, tied there, and her very dress spotted with him, but she never wanted courage, did Miss Mary Fraser of Adelaide and Lady Brackenstall of Abbey Grange hasn't learned new ways. You've questioned her long enough, you gentlemen, and now she is coming to her own room, just with her old Theresa, to get the rest that she badly needs.'

With a motherly tenderness the gaunt woman put her arm round her mistress and led her from the room.

'She has been with her all her life,' said Hopkins. 'Nursed her as a baby, and came with her to England when they first left Australia, eighteen months ago. Theresa Wright is her name, and the kind of maid you don't pick up nowadays. This way, Mr Holmes, if you please!'

The keen interest had passed out of Holmes's expressive face, and I knew that with the mystery all the charm of the case had departed. There still remained an arrest to be effected, but what were these commonplace rogues that he should soil his hands with them? An abstruse and learned specialist who finds that he has been called in for a case of measles would experience something of the annoyance which I read in my friend's eyes. Yet the scene in the dining room of the Abbey Grange was sufficiently strange to arrest his attention and to recall his waning interest.

It was a very large and high chamber, with carved oak ceiling, oaken panelling, and a fine array of deer's heads and ancient weapons around the walls. At the further end from the door was the high French window of which we had heard. Three smaller windows on the right-hand side filled the apartment with cold winter sunshine. On the left was a large, deep fireplace, with a massive, overhanging oak mantelpiece. Beside the fireplace was a heavy oaken chair with arms and cross-bars at the bottom. In and out through the open woodwork was woven a crimson cord, which was secured at each side to the crosspiece below. In releasing the lady, the cord had been slipped off her, but the knots with which it had been secured still remained. These details only struck our attention afterwards, for our thoughts were entirely absorbed by the terrible object which lay upon the tiger-skin hearthrug in front of the fire.

It was the body of a tall, well-made man, about forty years of age. He lay upon his back, his face upturned, with his white teeth grinning through his short black beard. His two clenched hands were raised above his head, and a heavy blackthorn stick lay across them. His dark, handsome, aquiline features were convulsed into a spasm of vindictive hatred, which had set his dead face in a terribly fiendish expression. He had evidently been in his bed when the alarm had broken out, for he wore a foppish embroidered night-shirt, and his bare feet projected from his trousers. His head was horribly injured, and the whole room bore witness to the savage ferocity of the blow which had struck him down. Beside him lay the heavy poker, bent into a curve by the concussion. Holmes examined both it and the indescribable wreck which it had wrought.

'He must be a powerful man, this elder Randall,' he remarked.

'Yes,' said Hopkins. 'I have some record of the fellow, and he is a rough customer.'

'You should have no difficulty in getting him.'

'Not the slightest. We have been on the lookout for him, and there was some idea that he had got away to America. Now that we know that the gang are here, I don't see how they can escape. We have the news at every seaport already, and a reward will be offered before evening. What beats me is how they could have done so mad a thing, knowing that the lady could describe them and that we could not fail to recognise the description.'

'Exactly. One would have expected that they would silence Lady Brackenstall as well.'

'They may not have realised,' I suggested, 'that she had recovered from her faint.'

'That is likely enough. If she seemed to be senseless, they would not take her life. What about this poor fellow, Hopkins? I seem to have heard some queer stories about him.'

'He was a good-hearted man when he was sober, but a perfect fiend when he was drunk, or rather when he was half drunk, for he seldom really went the whole way. The devil seemed to be in him at such times, and he was capable of anything. From what I hear, in spite of all his wealth and his title, he very nearly came our way once or twice. There was a scandal about his drenching a dog with petroleum and setting it on fire – her ladyship's dog, to make the matter worse – and that was only hushed up with difficulty. Then he threw a decanter at that maid, Theresa Wright – there was trouble about that. On the whole, and between ourselves, it will be a brighter house without him. What are you looking at now?'

Holmes was down on his knees, examining with great attention the knots upon the red cord with which the lady had been secured. Then he carefully scrutinised the broken and frayed end where it had snapped off when the burglar had dragged it down.

'When this was pulled down, the bell in the kitchen must have rung loudly,' he remarked.

'No one could hear it. The kitchen stands right at the back of the house.'

'How did the burglar know no one would hear it? How dared he pull at a bell-rope in that reckless fashion?'

'Exactly, Mr Holmes, exactly. You put the very question which I have asked myself again and again. There can be no doubt that this fellow must have known the house and its habits. He must have perfectly understood that the servants would all be in bed at that comparatively early hour, and that no one could possibly hear a bell ring in the kitchen. Therefore, he must have been in close league with one of the servants. Surely that is evident. But there are eight servants, and all of good character.'

'Other things being equal,' said Holmes, 'one would suspect the one at whose head the master threw a decanter. And yet that would involve treachery towards the mistress to whom this woman seems devoted. Well, well, the point is a minor one, and when you have Randall you will probably find no difficulty in securing his accomplice. The lady's story certainly seems to be corroborated, if it needed corroboration, by every detail which we see before us.' He walked to the French window and threw it open. 'There are no signs here, but the ground is iron hard, and one would not expect them. I see that these candles in the mantelpiece have been lighted.'

'Yes, it was by their light and that of the lady's bedroom candle, that the burglars saw their way about.'

'And what did they take?'

'Well, they did not take much – only half a dozen articles of plate off the sideboard. Lady Brackenstall thinks that they were themselves so disturbed by the death of Sir Eustace that they did not ransack the house, as they would otherwise have done.'

'No doubt that is true, and yet they drank some wine, I understand.'

'To steady their nerves.'

'Exactly. These three glasses upon the sideboard have been untouched, I suppose?'

'Yes, and the bottle stands as they left it.'

'Let us look at it. Halloa, halloa! What is this?'

The three glasses were grouped together, all of them tinged with wine, and one of them containing some dregs of beeswing. The bottle stood near them, two-thirds full, and beside it lay a long, deeply stained cork. Its appearance and the dust upon the bottle showed that it was no common vintage which the murderers had enjoyed.

A change had come over Holmes's manner. He had lost his listless expression, and again I saw an alert light of interest in his keen, deep-set eyes. He raised the cork and examined it minutely.

'How did they draw it?' he asked.

Hopkins pointed to a half-opened drawer. In it lay some table linen and a large corkscrew.

'Did Lady Brackenstall say that screw was used?'

'No, you remember that she was senseless at the moment when the bottle was opened.'

'Quite so. As a matter of fact, that screw was *not* used. This bottle was opened by a pocket screw, probably contained in a knife, and not more than an inch and a half long. If you will examine the top of the cork, you will observe that the screw was driven in three times before the cork was extracted. It has never been transfixed. This long screw would have transfixed it and drawn it up with a single pull. When you catch this fellow, you will find that he has one of these multiplex knives in his possession.'

'Excellent!' said Hopkins.

'But these glasses do puzzle me, I confess. Lady Brackenstall actually *saw* the three men drinking, did she not?'

'Yes; she was clear about that.'

'Then there is an end of it. What more is to be said? And yet, you must admit, that the three glasses are very remarkable, Hopkins. What? You see nothing remarkable? Well, well, let it pass. Perhaps, when a man has special knowledge and special powers like my own, it rather encourages him to seek a complex explanation when a simpler one is at hand. Of course, it must be a mere chance about the glasses. Well, good morning, Hopkins. I don't see that I can be of any use to you, and you appear to have your case very clear. You will let me know when Randall is arrested, and any further developments which may occur. I trust that I shall soon have to congratulate you upon a successful conclusion. Come, Watson, I fancy that we may employ ourselves more profitably at home.'

During our return journey, I could see by Holmes's

face that he was much puzzled by something which he had observed. Every now and then, by an effort, he would throw off the impression, and talk as if the matter were clear, but then his doubts would settle down upon him again, and his knitted brows and abstracted eyes would show that his thoughts had gone back once more to the great dining room of the Abbey Grange, in which this midnight tragedy had been enacted. At last, by a sudden impulse, just as our train was crawling out of a suburban station, he sprang on to the platform and pulled me out after him.

'Excuse me, my dear fellow,' said he, as we watched the rear carriages of our train disappearing round a curve, 'I am sorry to make you the victim of what may seem a mere whim, but on my life, Watson, I simply *can't* leave that case in this condition. Every instinct that I possess cries out against it. It's wrong – it's all wrong – I'll swear that it's wrong. And yet the lady's story was complete, the maid's corroboration was sufficient, the detail was fairly exact. What have I to put up against that? Three wine glasses, that is all. But if I had not taken things for granted, if I had examined everything with the care which I should have shown had we approached the case *de novo* and had no cut-and-dried story to warp my mind, should I not then have found something more definite to go upon? Of course I should. Sit down on this bench, Watson, until a train for Chislehurst arrives, and allow me to lay the evidence before you, imploring you in the first instance to dismiss from your mind the idea that anything which the maid or her mistress may have said must necessarily be true. The lady's charming personality must not be permitted to warp our judgment.

'Surely there are details in her story which, if we looked at in cold blood, would excite our suspicion. These burglars made a considerable haul at Sydenham a fortnight ago. Some account of them and of their appearance was in the papers, and would naturally occur to anyone who wished to invent a story in which imaginary robbers should play a part. As a matter of fact, burglars who have done a good stroke of business are, as a rule, only too glad to enjoy the proceeds in peace and quiet without embarking on another perilous undertaking. Again, it is unusual for burglars to operate at so early an hour, it is unusual for burglars to strike a lady to prevent her screaming, since one would imagine that was the sure way to make her scream, it is unusual for them to commit murder when their numbers are sufficient to overpower one man, it is unusual for them to be content with a limited plunder when there was much more within their reach, and finally, I should say, that it was very unusual for such men to leave a bottle half empty. How do all these unusuals strike you, Watson?'

'Their cumulative effect is certainly considerable, and yet each of them is quite possible in itself. The most unusual thing of all, as it seems to me, is that the lady should be tied to the chair.'

'Well, I am not so clear about that, Watson, for it is evident that they must either kill her or else secure her in such a way that she could not give immediate notice of their escape. But at any rate I have shown, have I not, that there is a certain element of improbability about the lady's story? And now, on the top of this, comes the incident of the wine glasses.'

'What about the wine glasses?'

'Can you see them in your mind's eye?'

'I see them clearly.'

'We are told that three men drank from them. Does that strike you as likely?'

'Why not? There was wine in each glass.'

'Exactly, but there was beeswing only in one glass. You must have noticed that fact. What does that suggest to your mind?'

'The last glass filled would be most likely to contain beeswing.'

'Not at all. The bottle was full of it, and it is inconceivable that the first two glasses were clear and the third heavily charged with it. There are two possible explanations, and only two. One is that after the second glass was filled the bottle was violently agitated, and so the third glass received the beeswing. That does not appear probable. No, no, I am sure that I am right.'

'What, then, do you suppose?'

'That only two glasses were used, and that the dregs of both were poured into a third glass, so as to give the false impression that three people had been here. In that way all the beeswing would be in the last glass, would it not? Yes, I am convinced that this is so. But if I have hit upon the true explanation of this one small phenomenon, then in an instant the case rises from the commonplace to the exceedingly remarkable, for it can only mean that Lady Brackenstall and her maid have deliberately lied to us, that not one word of their story is to be believed, that they have some very strong reason for covering the real criminal, and that we must construct our case for ourselves without any help from them.

That is the mission which now lies before us, and here, Watson, is the Sydenham train.'

The household at the Abbey Grange were much surprised at our return, but Sherlock Holmes, finding that Stanley Hopkins had gone off to report to headquarters, took possession of the dining room, locked the door upon the inside, and devoted himself for two hours to one of those minute and laborious investigations which form the solid basis on which his brilliant edifices of deduction were reared. Seated in a corner like an interested student who observes the demonstration of his professor, I followed every step of that remarkable research. The window, the curtains, the carpet, the chair, the rope – each in turn was minutely examined and duly pondered. The body of the unfortunate baronet had been removed, and all else remained as we had seen it in the morning. Finally, to my astonishment, Holmes climbed up on to the massive mantelpiece. Far above his head hung the few inches of red cord which were still attached to the wire. For a long time he gazed upward at it, and then in an attempt to get nearer to it he rested his knee upon a wooden bracket on the wall. This brought his hand within a few inches of the broken end of the rope, but it was not this so much as the bracket itself which seemed to engage his attention. Finally, he sprang down with an ejaculation of satisfaction.

'It's all right, Watson,' said he. 'We have got our case – one of the most remarkable in our collection. But, dear me, how slow-witted I have been, and how nearly I have committed the blunder of my lifetime! Now, I think that, with a few missing links, my chain is almost complete.'

'You have got your men?'

'Man, Watson, man. Only one, but a very formidable person. Strong as a lion – witness the blow that bent that poker! Six foot three in height, active as a squirrel, dexterous with his fingers, finally, remarkably quick-witted, for this whole ingenious story is of his concoction. Yes, Watson, we have come upon the handiwork of a very remarkable individual. And yet, in that bell-rope, he has given us a clue which should not have left us a doubt.'

'Where was the clue?'

'Well, if you were to pull down a bell-rope, Watson, where would you expect it to break? Surely at the spot where it is attached to the wire. Why should it break three inches from the top, as this one has done?'

'Because it is frayed there?'

'Exactly. This end, which we can examine, is frayed. He was cunning enough to do that with his knife. But the other end is not frayed. You could not observe that from here, but if you were on the mantelpiece you would see that it is cut clean off without any mark of fraying whatever. You can reconstruct what occurred. The man needed the rope. He would not tear it down for fear of giving the alarm by ringing the bell. What did he do? He sprang up on the mantelpiece, could not quite reach it, put his knee on the bracket – you will see the impression in the dust – and so got his knife to bear upon the cord. I could not reach the place by at least three inches – from which I infer that he is at least three inches a bigger man than I. Look at that mark upon the seat of the oaken chair! What is it?'

'Blood.'

'Undoubtedly it is blood. This alone puts the lady's story

out of court. If she were seated on the chair when the crime was done, how comes that mark? No, no, she was placed in the chair *after* the death of her husband. I'll wager that the black dress shows a corresponding mark to this. We have not yet met our Waterloo, Watson, but this is our Marengo, for it begins in defeat and ends in victory. I should like now to have a few words with the nurse, Theresa. We must be wary for a while, if we are to get the information which we want.'

She was an interesting person, this stern Australian nurse – taciturn, suspicious, ungracious, it took some time before Holmes's pleasant manner and frank acceptance of all that she said thawed her into a corresponding amiability. She did not attempt to conceal her hatred for her late employer.

'Yes, sir, it is true that he threw the decanter at me. I heard him call my mistress a name, and I told him that he would not dare to speak so if her brother had been there. Then it was that he threw it at me. He might have thrown a dozen if he had but left my bonny bird alone. He was forever ill-treating her, and she too proud to complain. She will not even tell me all that he has done to her. She never told me of those marks on her arm that you saw this morning, but I know very well that they come from a stab with a hatpin. The sly devil – God forgive me that I should speak of him so, now that he is dead! But a devil he was, if ever one walked the earth. He was all honey when first we met him – only eighteen months ago, and we both feel as if it were eighteen years. She had only just arrived in London. Yes, it was her first voyage – she had never been from home before. He won her with his title and his money and his false London ways. If she made a mistake she has paid for it, if ever a woman did. What month did we meet him? Well, I tell you it was just after we arrived. We arrived in June, and it was July. They were married in January of last year. Yes, she is down in the morning room again, and I have no doubt she will see you, but you must not ask too much of her, for she has gone through all that flesh and blood will stand.'

Lady Brackenstall was reclining on the same couch, but looked brighter than before. The maid had entered with us, and began once more to foment the bruise upon her mistress's brow.

'I hope,' said the lady, 'that you have not come to cross-examine me again?'

'No,' Holmes answered, in his gentlest voice, 'I will not cause you any unnecessary trouble, Lady Brackenstall, and my whole desire is to make things easy for you, for I am convinced that you are a much-tried woman. If you will treat me as a friend and trust me, you may find that I will justify your trust.'

'What do you want me to do?'

'To tell me the truth.'

'Mr Holmes!'

'No, no, Lady Brackenstall – it is no use. You may have heard of any little reputation which I possess. I will stake it all on the fact that your story is an absolute fabrication.'

Mistress and maid were both staring at Holmes with pale faces and frightened eyes.

'You are an impudent fellow!' cried Theresa. 'Do you mean to say that my mistress has told a lie?'

Holmes rose from his chair.

'Have you nothing to tell me?'

'I have told you everything.'

'Think once more, Lady Brackenstall. Would it not be better to be frank?'

For an instant there was hesitation in her beautiful face. Then some new strong thought caused it to set like a mask.

'I have told you all I know.'

Holmes took his hat and shrugged his shoulders. 'I am sorry,' he said, and without another word we left the room and the house. There was a pond in the park, and to this my friend led the way. It was frozen over, but a single hole was left for the convenience of a solitary swan. Holmes gazed at it, and then passed on to the lodge gate. There he scribbled a short note for Stanley Hopkins, and left it with the lodge-keeper.

'It may be a hit, or it may be a miss, but we are bound to do something for friend Hopkins, just to justify this second visit,' said he. 'I will not quite take him into my confidence yet. I think our next scene of operations must be the shipping office of the Adelaide–Southampton line, which stands at the end of Pall Mall, if I remember right. There is a second line of steamers which connect South Australia with England, but we will draw the larger cover first.'

Holmes's card sent in to the manager ensured instant attention, and he was not long in acquiring all the information he needed. In June of '95, only one of their line had reached a home port. It was the *Rock of Gibraltar*, their largest and best boat. A reference to the passenger list showed that Miss Fraser, of Adelaide, with her maid had made the voyage in her. The boat was now somewhere south of the Suez Canal on her way to Australia. Her officers were the same as in

'95, with one exception. The first officer, Mr Jack Crocker, had been made a captain and was to take charge of their new ship, the *Bass Rock*, sailing in two days' time from Southampton. He lived at Sydenham, but he was likely to be in that morning for instructions, if we cared to wait for him.

No, Mr Holmes had no desire to see him, but would be glad to know more about his record and character.

His record was magnificent. There was not an officer in the fleet to touch him. As to his character, he was reliable on duty, but a wild, desperate fellow off the deck of his ship – hot-headed, excitable, but loyal, honest and kind-hearted. That was the pith of the information with which Holmes left the office of the Adelaide–Southampton company. Thence he drove to Scotland Yard, but, instead of entering, he sat in his cab with his brows drawn down, lost in profound thought. Finally he drove round to the Charing Cross telegraph office, sent off a message, and then, at last, we made for Baker Street once more.

'No, I couldn't do it, Watson,' said he, as we re-entered our room. 'Once that warrant was made out, nothing on earth would save him. Once or twice in my career I feel that I have done more real harm by my discovery of the criminal than ever he had done by his crime. I have learned caution now, and I had rather play tricks with the law of England than with my own conscience. Let us know a little more before we act.'

Before evening, we had a visit from Inspector Stanley Hopkins. Things were not going very well with him.

'I believe that you are a wizard, Mr Holmes. I really do sometimes think that you have powers that are not human.

Now, how on earth could you know that the stolen silver was at the bottom of that pond?'

'I didn't know it.'

'But you told me to examine it.'

'You got it, then?'

'Yes, I got it.'

'I am very glad if I have helped you.'

'But you haven't helped me. You have made the affair far more difficult. What sort of burglars are they who steal silver and then throw it into the nearest pond?'

'It was certainly rather eccentric behaviour. I was merely going on the idea that if the silver had been taken by persons who did not want it – who merely took it for a blind, as it were – then they would naturally be anxious to get rid of it.'

'But why should such an idea cross your mind?'

'Well, I thought it was possible. When they came out through the French window, there was the pond with one tempting little hole in the ice, right in front of their noses. Could there be a better hiding place?'

'Ah, a hiding place – that is better!' cried Stanley Hopkins. 'Yes, yes, I see it all now! It was early, there were folk upon the roads, they were afraid of being seen with the silver, so they sank it in the pond, intending to return for it when the coast was clear. Excellent, Mr Holmes – that is better than your idea of a blind.'

'Quite so, you have got an admirable theory. I have no doubt that my own ideas were quite wild, but you must admit that they have ended in discovering the silver.'

'Yes, sir – yes. It was all your doing. But I have had a bad setback.'

'A setback?'

'Yes, Mr Holmes. The Randall gang were arrested in New York this morning.'

'Dear me, Hopkins! That is certainly rather against your theory that they committed a murder in Kent last night.'

'It is fatal, Mr Holmes – absolutely fatal. Still, there are other gangs of three besides the Randalls, or it may be some new gang of which the police have never heard.'

'Quite so, it is perfectly possible. What, are you off?'

'Yes, Mr Holmes, there is no rest for me until I have got to the bottom of the business. I suppose you have no hint to give me?'

'I have given you one.'

'Which?'

'Well, I suggested a blind.'

'But why, Mr Holmes, why?'

'Ah, that's the question, of course. But I commend the idea to your mind. You might possibly find that there was something in it. You won't stop for dinner? Well, goodbye, and let us know how you get on.'

Dinner was over, and the table cleared before Holmes alluded to the matter again. He had lit his pipe and held his slippered feet to the cheerful blaze of the fire. Suddenly he looked at his watch.

'I expect developments, Watson.'

'When?'

'Now – within a few minutes. I dare say you thought I acted rather badly to Stanley Hopkins just now?'

'I trust your judgment.'

'A very sensible reply, Watson. You must look at it this

way: what I know is unofficial, what he knows is official. I have the right to private judgment, but he has none. He must disclose all, or he is a traitor to his service. In a doubtful case I would not put him in so painful a position, and so I reserve my information until my own mind is clear upon the matter.'

'But when will that be?'

'The time has come. You will now be present at the last scene of a remarkable little drama.'

There was a sound upon the stairs, and our door was opened to admit as fine a specimen of manhood as ever passed through it. He was a very tall young man, golden-moustached, blue-eyed, with a skin which had been burned by tropical suns, and a springy step, which showed that the huge frame was as active as it was strong. He closed the door behind him, and then he stood with clenched hands and heaving breast, choking down some overmastering emotion.

'Sit down, Captain Crocker. You got my telegram?'

Our visitor sank into an armchair and looked from one to the other of us with questioning eyes.

'I got your telegram, and I came at the hour you said. I heard that you had been down to the office. There was no getting away from you. Let's hear the worst. What are you going to do with me? Arrest me? Speak out, man! You can't sit there and play with me like a cat with a mouse.'

'Give him a cigar,' said Holmes. 'Bite on that, Captain Crocker, and don't let your nerves run away with you. I should not sit here smoking with you if I thought that you were a common criminal, you may be sure of that. Be frank with me and we may do some good. Play tricks with me, and I'll crush you.'

'What do you wish me to do?'

'To give me a true account of all that happened at the Abbey Grange last night – a *true* account, mind you, with nothing added and nothing taken off. I know so much already that if you go one inch off the straight, I'll blow this police whistle from my window and the affair goes out of my hands forever.'

The sailor thought for a little. Then he struck his leg with his great sunburned hand.

'I'll chance it,' he cried. 'I believe you are a man of your word, and a white man, and I'll tell you the whole story. But one thing I will say first. So far as I am concerned, I regret nothing and I fear nothing, and I would do it all again and be proud of the job. Damn the beast, if he had as many lives as a cat, he would owe them all to me! But it's the lady, Mary – Mary Fraser – for never will I call her by that accursed name. When I think of getting her into trouble, I who would give my life just to bring one smile to her dear face, it's that that turns my soul into water. And yet – and yet – what less could I do? I'll tell you my story, gentlemen, and then I'll ask you, as man to man, what less could I do?

'I must go back a bit. You seem to know everything, so I expect that you know that I met her when she was a passenger and I was first officer of the *Rock of Gibraltar.* From the first day I met her, she was the only woman to me. Every day of that voyage I loved her more, and many a time since have I kneeled down in the darkness of the night watch and kissed the deck of that ship because I knew her dear feet had trod it. She was never engaged to me. She treated me as fairly as ever a woman treated a man. I have no complaint to make. It was all love on my side, and all good comradeship and friendship on hers. When we parted she was a free woman, but I could never again be a free man.

'Next time I came back from sea, I heard of her marriage. Well, why shouldn't she marry whom she liked? Title and money – who could carry them better than she? She was born for all that is beautiful and dainty. I didn't grieve over her marriage. I was not such a selfish hound as that. I just rejoiced that good luck had come her way, and that she had not thrown herself away on a penniless sailor. That's how I loved Mary Fraser.

'Well, I never thought to see her again, but last voyage I was promoted, and the new boat was not yet launched, so I had to wait for a couple of months with my people at Sydenham. One day out in a country lane I met Theresa Wright, her old maid. She told me all about her, about him, about everything. I tell you, gentlemen, it nearly drove me mad. This drunken hound, that he should dare to raise his hand to her, whose boots he was not worthy to lick! I met Theresa again. Then I met Mary herself – and met her again. Then she would meet me no more. But the other day I had a notice that I was to start on my voyage within a week, and I determined that I would see her once before I left. Theresa was always my friend, for she loved Mary and hated this villain almost as much as I did. From her I learned the ways of the house. Mary used to sit up reading in her own little room downstairs. I crept round there last night and scratched at the window. At first she would not open to me, but in her heart I know that now she loves me, and she could not leave me in the frosty night. She whispered to me to come round to the big front window, and I found it open before me, so as to let me into the dining room. Again I heard from her own lips things that made my blood boil, and again I cursed this brute who mishandled the woman I loved. Well, gentlemen, I was standing with her just inside the window, in all innocence, as God is my judge, when he rushed like a madman into the room, called her the vilest name that a man could use to a woman, and welted her across the face with the stick he had in his hand. I had sprung for the poker, and it was a fair fight between us. See here, on my arm, where his first blow fell. Then it was my turn, and I went through him as if he had been a rotten pumpkin. Do you think I was sorry? Not I! It was his life or mine, but far more than that, it was his life or hers, for how could I leave her in the power of this madman? That was how I killed him. Was I wrong? Well, then, what would either of you gentlemen have done, if you had been in my position?

'She had screamed when he struck her, and that brought old Theresa down from the room above. There was a bottle of wine on the sideboard, and I opened it and poured a little between Mary's lips, for she was half dead with shock. Then I took a drop myself. Theresa was as cool as ice, and it was her plot as much as mine. We must make it appear that burglars had done the thing. Theresa kept on repeating our story to her mistress, while I swarmed up and cut the rope of the bell. Then I lashed her in her chair, and frayed out the end of the rope to make it look natural, else they would wonder how in the world a burglar could have got up there to cut it. Then I gathered up a few plates and pots of silver, to carry out the idea of the robbery, and there I left them, with orders to give the alarm when I had a quarter of an hour's start. I dropped the silver into the pond, and made off for Sydenham, feeling that for once in my life I had done a real good night's work. And that's the truth and the whole truth, Mr Holmes, if it costs me my neck.'

Holmes smoked for some time in silence. Then he crossed the room, and shook our visitor by the hand.

'That's what I think,' said he. 'I know that every word is true, for you have hardly said a word which I did not know. No one but an acrobat or a sailor could have got up to that bell-rope from the bracket, and no one but a sailor could have made the knots with which the cord was fastened to the chair. Only once had this lady been brought into contact with sailors, and that was on her voyage, and it was someone of her own class of life, since she was trying hard to shield him, and so showing that she loved him. You see how easy it was for me to lay my hands upon you when once I had started upon the right trail.'

'I thought the police never could have seen through our dodge.'

'And the police haven't, nor will they, to the best of my belief. Now, look here, Captain Crocker, this is a very serious matter, though I am willing to admit that you acted under the most extreme provocation to which any man could be subjected. I am not sure that in defence of your own life your action will not be pronounced legitimate. However, that is for a British jury to decide. Meanwhile I have so much sympathy for you that, if you choose to disappear in the next twenty-four hours, I will promise you that no one will hinder you.'

'And then it will all come out?'

'Certainly it will come out.'

The sailor flushed with anger.

'What sort of proposal is that to make a man? I know enough of law to understand that Mary would be held as accomplice. Do you think I would leave her alone to face the music while I slunk away? No, sir, let them do their worst upon me, but for Heaven's sake, Mr Holmes, find some way of keeping my poor Mary out of the courts.'

Holmes for a second time held out his hand to the sailor.

'I was only testing you, and you ring true every time. Well, it is a great responsibility that I take upon myself, but I have given Hopkins an excellent hint and if he can't avail himself of it I can do no more. See here, Captain Crocker, we'll do this in due form of law. You are the prisoner. Watson, you are a British jury, and I never met a man who was more eminently fitted to represent one. I am the judge. Now, gentleman of the jury, you have heard the evidence. Do you find the prisoner guilty or not guilty?'

'Not guilty, my lord,' said I.

'*Vox populi, vox Dei*. You are acquitted, Captain Crocker. So long as the law does not find some other victim you are safe from me. Come back to this lady in a year, and may her future and yours justify us in the judgment which we have pronounced this night!'

The Mystery of Felwyn Tunnel

L. T. Meade and Robert Eustace

I was making experiments of some interest at South Kensington, and hoped that I had perfected a small but not unimportant discovery, when, on returning home one evening in late October in the year 1893, I found a visiting card on my table. On it were inscribed the words, 'Mr Geoffrey Bainbridge'. This name was quite unknown to me, so I rang the bell and inquired of my servant who the visitor had been. He described him as a gentleman who wished to see me on most urgent business, and said further that Mr Bainbridge intended to call again later in the evening. It was with both curiosity and vexation that I awaited the return of the stranger. Urgent business with me generally meant a hurried rush to one part of the country or the other. I did not want to leave London just then; and when at half-past nine Mr Geoffrey Bainbridge was ushered into my room, I received him with a certain coldness which he could not fail to perceive. He was a tall, well-dressed, elderly man. He immediately plunged into the object of his visit.

'I hope you do not consider my unexpected presence an intrusion, Mr Bell,' he said. 'But I have heard of you from our mutual friends, the Greys of Uplands. You may remember once doing that family a great service.'

'I remember perfectly well,' I answered more cordially. 'Pray tell me what you want; I shall listen with attention.'

'I believe you are the one man in London who can help me,' he continued. 'I refer to a matter especially relating to your own particular study. I need hardly say that whatever you do will not be unrewarded.'

'That is neither here nor there,' I said; 'but before you go any further, allow me to ask one question. Do you want me to leave London at present?'

He raised his eyebrows in dismay.

'I certainly do,' he answered.

'Very well; pray proceed with your story.'

He looked at me with anxiety.

'In the first place,' he began, 'I must tell you that I am chairman of the Lytton Vale Railway Company in Wales, and that it is on an important matter connected with our line that I have come to consult you. When I explain to you the nature of the mystery, you will not wonder, I think, at my soliciting your aid.'

'I will give you my closest attention,' I answered; and then I added, impelled to say the latter words by a certain expression on his face, 'if I can see my way to assisting you I shall be ready to do so.'

'Pray accept my cordial thanks,' he replied. 'I have come up from my place at Felwyn today on purpose to consult you. It is in that neighbourhood that the affair has occurred. As it is essential that you should be in possession of the facts of the whole matter, I will go over things just as they happened.'

I bent forward and listened attentively.

'This day fortnight,' continued Mr Bainbridge, 'our quiet little village was horrified by the news that the signalman on duty at the mouth of the Felwyn Tunnel had been found dead under the most mysterious circumstances. The tunnel is at the end of a long cutting between Llanlys and Felwyn stations. It is about a mile long, and the signal box is on the Felwyn side. The place is extremely lonely, being six miles from the village across the mountains. The name of the poor fellow who met his death in this mysterious fashion was David Pritchard. I have known him from a boy, and he was quite one of the steadiest and most trustworthy men on the line. On Tuesday evening he went on duty at six o'clock; on Wednesday morning the day-man who had come to relieve him was surprised not to find him in the box. It was just getting daylight, and the 6.30 local was coming down, so he pulled the signals and let her through. Then he went out, and, looking up the line towards the tunnel, saw Pritchard lying beside the line close to the mouth of the tunnel. Roberts, the day-man, ran up to him and found, to his horror, that he was quite dead. At first Roberts naturally supposed that he had been cut down by a train, as there was a wound at the back of the head; but he was not lying on the metals. Roberts ran back to the box and telegraphed through to Felwyn Station. The message was sent on to the village, and at half-past seven o'clock the police inspector came up to my house with the news. He and I, with the local doctor, went off at once to the tunnel. We found the dead man lying beside the metals a few yards away from the mouth of the tunnel, and the doctor immediately gave him a careful examination. There was a depressed fracture at the back of the skull, which must have caused his death; but how he came by it was not so clear. On examining the whole place most carefully, we saw, further, that there were marks on the rocks at the steep side of the embankment as if someone had tried to scramble up them. Why the poor fellow had attempted such a climb, God only knows. In doing so he must have slipped and fallen back on to the line, thus causing the fracture of the skull. In no case could he have gone up more than eight or ten feet, as the banks of the cutting run sheer up, almost perpendicularly, beyond that point for more than a hundred and fifty feet. There are some sharp boulders beside the line, and it was possible that he might have fallen on one of these and so sustained the injury. The affair must have occurred some time between 11.45 pm and 6 am, as the engine-driver of the express at 11.45 pm states that the line was signalled clear, and he also caught sight of Pritchard in his box as he passed.'

'This is deeply interesting,' I said; 'pray proceed.'

Bainbridge looked at me earnestly; he then continued:

'The whole thing is shrouded in mystery. Why should Pritchard have left his box and gone down to the tunnel? Why, having done so, should he have made a wild attempt to scale the side of the cutting, an impossible feat at any time?

Had danger threatened, the ordinary course of things would have been to run up the line towards the signal box. These points are quite unexplained. Another curious fact is that death appears to have taken place just before the day-man came on duty, as the light at the mouth of the tunnel had been put out, and it was one of the night signalman's duties to do this as soon as daylight appeared; it is possible, therefore, that Pritchard went down to the tunnel for that purpose. Against this theory, however, and an objection that seems to nullify it, is the evidence of Dr Williams, who states that when he examined the body his opinion was that death had taken place some hours before. An inquest was held on the following day, but before it took place there was a new and most important development. I now come to what I consider the crucial point in the whole story.

'For a long time there had been a feud between Pritchard and another man of the name of Wynne, a platelayer on the line. The object of their quarrel was the blacksmith's daughter in the neighbouring village – a remarkably pretty girl and an arrant flirt. Both men were madly in love with her, and she played them off one against the other. The night but one before his death Pritchard and Wynne had met at the village inn, had quarrelled in the bar – Lucy, of course, being the subject of their difference. Wynne was heard to say (he was a man of powerful build and subject to fits of ungovernable rage) that he would have Pritchard's life. Pritchard swore a great oath that he would get Lucy on the following day to promise to marry him. This oath, it appears, he kept, and on his way to the signal box on Tuesday evening met Wynne, and triumphantly told him that Lucy had promised to be his wife. The men had a hand-to-hand fight on the spot, several people from the village being witnesses of it. They were separated with difficulty, each vowing vengeance on the other. Pritchard went off to his duty at the signal box and Wynne returned to the village to drown his sorrows at the public house.

'Very late that same night Wynne was seen by a villager going in the direction of the tunnel. The man stopped him and questioned him. He explained that he had left some of his tools on the line, and was on his way to fetch them. The villager noticed that he looked queer and excited, but not wishing to pick a quarrel thought it best not to question him further. It has been proved that Wynne never returned home that night, but came back at an early hour on the following morning, looking dazed and stupid. He was arrested on suspicion, and at the inquest the verdict was against him.'

'Has he given any explanation of his own movements?' I asked.

'Yes; but nothing that can clear him. As a matter of fact, his tools were nowhere to be seen on the line, nor did he bring them home with him. His own story is that being considerably the worse for drink, he had fallen down in one of the fields and slept there till morning.'

'Things look black against him,' I said.

'They do; but listen, I have something more to add. Here comes a very queer feature in the affair. Lucy Ray, the girl who had caused the feud between Pritchard and Wynne, after hearing the news of Pritchard's death, completely lost her head, and ran frantically about the village declaring that Wynne was the man she really loved, and that she had only accepted Pritchard in a fit of rage with Wynne for not himself bringing matters to the point. The case looks very bad against Wynne, and yesterday the magistrate committed him for trial at the coming assizes. The unhappy Lucy Ray and the young man's parents are in a state bordering on distraction.'

'What is your own opinion with regard to Wynne's guilt?' I asked.

'Before God, Mr Bell, I believe the poor fellow is innocent, but the evidence against him is very strong. One of the favourite theories is that he went down to the tunnel and extinguished the light, knowing that this would bring Pritchard out of his box to see what was the matter, and that he then attacked him, striking the blow which fractured the skull.'

'Has any weapon been found about, with which he could have given such a blow?'

'No; nor has anything of the kind been discovered on Wynne's person; that fact is decidedly in his favour.'

'But what about the marks on the rocks?' I asked.

'It is possible that Wynne may have made them in order to divert suspicion by making people think that Pritchard must have fallen, and so killed himself. The holders of this theory base their belief on the absolute want of cause for Pritchard's trying to scale the rock. The whole thing is the most absolute enigma. Some of the country folk have declared that the tunnel is haunted (and there certainly has been such a rumour current among them for years). That Pritchard saw some apparition, and in wild terror sought to escape from it by climbing the rocks, is another theory, but only the most imaginative hold it.'

'Well, it is a most extraordinary case,' I replied.

'Yes, Mr Bell, and I should like to get your opinion of it. Do you see your way to elucidate the mystery?'

'Not at present; but I shall be happy to investigate the matter to my utmost ability.'

'But you do not wish to leave London at present?'

'That is so; but a matter of such importance cannot be set aside. It appears, from what you say, that Wynne's life hangs more or less on my being able to clear away the mystery?'

'That is indeed the case. There ought not to be a single stone left unturned to get at the truth, for the sake of Wynne. Well, Mr Bell, what do you propose to do?'

'To see the place without delay,' I answered.

'That is right; when can you come?'

'Whenever you please.'

'Will you come down to Felwyn with me tomorrow? I shall leave Paddington by the 7.10, and if you will be my guest I shall be only too pleased to put you up.'

'That arrangement will suit me admirably,' I replied. 'I will meet you by the train you mention, and the affair shall have my best attention.'

'Thank you,' he said, rising. He shook hands with me and took his leave.

The next day I met Bainbridge at Paddington Station, and we were soon flying westward in the luxurious private compartment that had been reserved for him. I could see by his abstracted manner and his long lapses of silence that the mysterious affair at Felwyn Tunnel was occupying all his thoughts.

It was two o'clock in the afternoon when the train slowed

down at the little station of Felwyn. The stationmaster was at the door in an instant to receive us.

'I have some terribly bad news for you, sir,' he said, turning to Bainbridge as we alighted; 'and yet in one sense it is a relief, for it seems to clear Wynne.'

'What do you mean?' cried Bainbridge. 'Bad news? Speak out at once!'

'Well, sir, it is this; there has been another death at Felwyn signal box. John Davidson, who was on duty last night, was found dead at an early hour this morning in the very same place where we found poor Pritchard.'

'Good God!' cried Bainbridge, starting back, 'what an awful thing! What, in the name of Heaven, does it mean, Mr Bell? This is too fearful. Thank goodness you have come down with us.'

'It is as black a business as I ever heard of, sir,' echoed the stationmaster; 'and what we are to do I don't know. Poor Davidson was found dead this morning, and there was neither mark nor sign of what killed him – that is the extraordinary part of it. There's a perfect panic abroad, and not a signalman on the line will take duty tonight. I was quite in despair, and was afraid at one time that the line would have to be closed, but at last it occurred to me to wire to Lytton Vale, and they are sending down an inspector. I expect him by a special every moment. I believe this is he coming now,' added the stationmaster, looking up the line.

There was the sound of a whistle down the valley, and in a few moments a single engine shot into the station, and an official in uniform stepped on to the platform.

'Good evening, sir,' he said, touching his cap to

Bainbridge; 'I have just been sent down to inquire into this affair at the Felwyn Tunnel, and though it seems more of a matter for a Scotland Yard detective than one of ourselves, there was nothing for it but to come. All the same, Mr Bainbridge, I cannot say that I look forward to spending tonight alone at the place.'

'You wish for the services of a detective, but you shall have someone better,' said Bainbridge, turning towards me. 'This gentleman, Mr John Bell, is the man of all others for our business. I have just brought him down from London for the purpose.'

An expression of relief flitted across the inspector's face.

'I am very glad to see you, sir,' he said to me, 'and I hope you will be able to spend the night with me in the signal box. I must say I don't much relish the idea of tackling the thing single-handed; but with your help, sir, I think we ought to get to the bottom of it somehow. I am afraid there is not a man on the line who will take duty until we do. So it is most important that the thing should be cleared, and without delay.'

I readily assented to the inspector's proposition, and Bainbridge and I arranged that we should call for him at four o'clock at the village inn and drive him to the tunnel.

We then stepped into the waggonette which was waiting for us, and drove to Bainbridge's house.

Mrs Bainbridge came out to meet us, and was full of the tragedy. Two pretty girls also ran to greet their father, and to glance inquisitively at me. I could see that the entire family was in a state of much excitement.

'Lucy Ray has just left, father,' said the elder of the girls. 'We had much trouble to soothe her; she is in a frantic state.'

'You have heard, Mr Bell, all about this dreadful mystery?' said Mrs Bainbridge as she led me towards the dining room.

'Yes,' I answered; 'your husband has been good enough to give me every particular.'

'And you have really come here to help us?'

'I hope I may be able to discover the cause,' I answered.

'It certainly seems most extraordinary,' continued Mrs Bainbridge. 'My dear,' she continued, turning to her husband, 'you can easily imagine the state we were all in this morning when the news of the second death was brought to us.'

'For my part,' said Ella Bainbridge, 'I am sure that Felwyn Tunnel is haunted. The villagers have thought so for a long time, and this second death seems to prove it, does it not?' Here she looked anxiously at me.

'I can offer no opinion,' I replied, 'until I have sifted the matter thoroughly.'

'Come, Ella, don't worry Mr Bell,' said her father; 'if he is as hungry as I am, he must want his lunch.'

We then seated ourselves at the table and commenced the meal. Bainbridge, although he professed to be hungry, was in such a state of excitement that he could scarcely eat. Immediately after lunch he left me to the care of his family and went into the village.

'It is just like him,' said Mrs Bainbridge; 'he takes these sort of things to heart dreadfully. He is terribly upset about Lucy Ray, and also about the poor fellow Wynne. It is certainly a fearful tragedy from first to last.'

'Well, at any rate,' I said, 'this fresh death will upset the evidence against Wynne.'

'I hope so, and there is some satisfaction in the fact. Well, Mr Bell, I see you have finished lunch; will you come into the drawing room?'

I followed her into a pleasant room overlooking the valley of the Lytton.

By-and-by Bainbridge returned, and soon afterwards the dog-cart came to the door. My host and I mounted, Bainbridge took the reins, and we started off at a brisk pace.

'Matters get worse and worse,' he said the moment we were alone. 'If you don't clear things up tonight, Bell, I say frankly that I cannot imagine what will happen.'

We entered the village, and as we rattled down the ill-paved streets I was greeted with curious glances on all sides. The people were standing about in groups, evidently talking about the tragedy and nothing else. Suddenly, as our trap bumped noisily over the paving stones, a girl darted out of one of the houses and made frantic motions to Bainbridge to stop the horse. He pulled the mare nearly up on her haunches, and the girl came up to the side of the dog-cart.

'You have heard it?' she said, speaking eagerly and in a gasping voice. 'The death which occurred this morning will clear Stephen Wynne, won't it, Mr Bainbridge? It will, you are sure, are you not?'

'It looks like it, Lucy, my poor girl,' he answered. 'But there, the whole thing is so terrible that I scarcely know what to think.'

She was a pretty girl with dark eyes, and under ordinary circumstances must have had the vivacious expression of face and the brilliant complexion which so many of her countrywomen possess. But now her eyes were swollen with weeping and her complexion more or less disfigured by the agony she had gone through. She looked piteously at Bainbridge, her lips trembling. The next moment she burst into tears.

'Come away, Lucy,' said a woman who had followed her out of the cottage; 'Fie – for shame! Don't trouble the gentlemen; come back and stay quiet.'

'I can't, mother, I can't,' said the unfortunate girl. 'If they hang him, I'll go clean off my head. Oh, Mr Bainbridge, do say that the second death has cleared him!'

'I have every hope that it will do so, Lucy,' said Bainbridge, 'but now don't keep us, there's a good girl; go back into the house. This gentleman has come down from London on purpose to look into the whole matter. I may have good news for you in the morning.'

The girl raised her eyes to my face with a look of intense pleading. 'Oh, I have been cruel and a fool, and I deserve everything,' she gasped; 'but, sir, for the love of Heaven, try to clear him.'

I promised to do my best.

Bainbridge touched up the mare, she bounded forward, and Lucy disappeared into the cottage with her mother.

The next moment we drew up at the inn where the inspector was waiting, and soon afterwards were bowling along between the high banks of the country lanes to the tunnel. It was a cold, still afternoon; the air was wonderfully keen, for a sharp frost had held the countryside in its grip for the last two days. The sun was just tipping the hills to westward when the trap pulled up at the top of the cutting. We hastily alighted, and the inspector and I bade Bainbridge goodbye.

He said that he only wished that he could stay with us for the night, assured us that little sleep would visit him, and that he would be back at the cutting at an early hour on the following morning; then the noise of his horse's feet was heard fainter and fainter as he drove back over the frost-bound roads. The inspector and I ran along the little path to the wicket-gate in the fence, stamping our feet on the hard ground to restore circulation after our cold drive. The next moment we were looking down upon the scene of the mysterious deaths, and a weird and lonely place it looked. The tunnel was at one end of the rock cutting, the sides of which ran sheer down to the line for over a hundred and fifty feet. Above the tunnel's mouth the hills rose one upon the other. A more dreary place it would have been difficult to imagine. From a little clump of pines a delicate film of blue smoke rose straight up on the still air. This came from the chimney of the signal box.

As we started to descend the precipitous path the inspector sang out a cheery 'Hullo!' The man on duty in the box immediately answered. His voice echoed and reverberated down the cutting, and the next moment he appeared at the door of the box. He told us that he would be with us immediately; but we called back to him to stay where he was, and the next instant the inspector and I entered the box.

'The first thing to do,' said Henderson the inspector, 'is to send a message down the line to announce our arrival.'

This he did, and in a few moments a crawling goods train came panting up the cutting. After signalling her through we descended the wooden flight of steps which led from the box down to the line and walked along the metals towards the tunnel till we stood on the spot where poor Davidson had been found dead that morning. I examined the ground and all around it most carefully. Everything tallied exactly with the description I had received. There could be no possible way of approaching the spot except by going along the line, as the rocky sides of the cutting were inaccessible.

'It is a most extraordinary thing, sir,' said the signalman whom we had come to relieve. 'Davidson had neither mark nor sign on him – there he lay stone dead and cold, and not a bruise nowhere; but Pritchard had an awful wound at the back of the head. They said he got it by climbing the rocks – here, you can see the marks for yourself, sir. But now, is it likely that Pritchard would try to climb rocks like these, so steep as they are?'

'Certainly not,' I replied.

'Then how do you account for the wound, sir?' asked the man with an anxious face.

'I cannot tell you at present,' I answered.

'And you and Inspector Henderson are going to spend the night in the signal box?'

'Yes.'

A horrified expression crept over the signalman's face.

'God preserve you both,' he said; 'I wouldn't do it – not for fifty pounds. It's not the first time I have heard tell that Felwyn Tunnel is haunted. But, there, I won't say any more about that. It's a black business, and has given trouble enough. There's poor Wynne, the same thing as convicted of the murder of Pritchard; but now they say that Davidson's death will clear him. Davidson was as good a fellow as you would come across this side of the country; but for the matter of that, so was Pritchard. The whole thing is terrible – it upsets one, that it do, sir.'

'I don't wonder at your feelings,' I answered; 'but now, see here, I want to make a most careful examination of everything. One of the theories is that Wynne crept down this rocky side and fractured Pritchard's skull. I believe such a feat to be impossible. On examining these rocks I see that a man might climb up the side of the tunnel as far as from eight to ten feet, utilising the sharp projections of rock for the purpose; but it would be out of the question for any man to come down the cutting. No; the only way Wynne could have approached Pritchard was by the line itself. But, after all, the real thing to discover is this,' I continued: 'what killed Davidson? Whatever caused his death is, beyond doubt, equally responsible for Pritchard's. I am now going into the tunnel.'

Inspector Henderson went in with me. The place struck damp and chill. The walls were covered with green, evil-smelling fungi, and through the brickwork the moisture was oozing and had trickled down in long lines to the ground. Before us was nothing but dense darkness.

When we reappeared the signalman was lighting the red lamp on the post, which stood about five feet from the ground just above the entrance to the tunnel.

'Is there plenty of oil?' asked the inspector.

'Yes, sir, plenty,' replied the man. 'Is there anything more I can do for either of you gentlemen?' he asked, pausing, and evidently dying to be off.

'Nothing,' answered Henderson; 'I will wish you good evening.'

'Good evening to you both,' said the man. He made his way quickly up the path and was soon lost to sight.

Henderson and I then returned to the signal box.

By this time it was nearly dark.

'How many trains pass in the night?' I asked of the inspector.

'There's the 10.20 down express,' he said, 'it will pass here at about 10.40; then there's the 11.45 up, and then not another train till the 6.30 local tomorrow morning. We shan't have a very lively time,' he added.

I approached the fire and bent over it, holding out my hands to try and get some warmth into them.

'It will take a good deal to persuade me to go down to the tunnel, whatever I may see there,' said the man. 'I don't think, Mr Bell, I am a coward in any sense of the word, but there's something very uncanny about this place, right away from the rest of the world. I don't wonder one often hears of signalmen going mad in some of these lonely boxes. Have you any theory to account for these deaths, sir?'

'None at present,' I replied.

'This second death puts the idea of Pritchard being murdered quite out of court,' he continued.

'I am sure of it,' I answered.

'And so am I, and that's one comfort,' continued Henderson. 'That poor girl, Lucy Ray, although she was to be blamed for her conduct, is much to be pitied now; and as to poor Wynne himself, he protests his innocence through thick and thin. He was a wild fellow, but not the sort to take the life of a fellow-creature. I saw the doctor this afternoon while I was waiting for you at the inn, Mr Bell, and also the police sergeant. They both say they do not know what Davidson died of. There was not the least sign of violence on the body.'

'Well, I am as puzzled as the rest of you,' I said. 'I have one or two theories in my mind, but none of them will quite fit the situation.'

The night was piercingly cold, and, although there was not a breath of wind, the keen and frosty air penetrated into the lonely signal box. We spoke little, and both of us were doubtless absorbed by our own thoughts and speculations. As to Henderson, he looked distinctly uncomfortable, and I cannot say that my own feelings were too pleasant. Never had I been given a tougher problem to solve, and never had I been so utterly at my wits' end for a solution.

Now and then the inspector got up and went to the telegraph instrument, which intermittently clicked away in its box. As he did so he made some casual remark and then sat down again. After the 10.40 had gone through, there followed a period of silence which seemed almost oppressive. All at once the stillness was broken by the whirr of the electric bell, which sounded so sharply in our ears that we both started. Henderson rose.

'That's the 11.45 coming,' he said, and, going over to the three long levers, he pulled two of them down with a loud clang. The next moment, with a rush and a scream, the express tore down the cutting, the carriage lights streamed past in a rapid flash, the ground trembled, a few sparks from the engine whirled up into the darkness, and the train plunged into the tunnel.

'And now,' said Henderson, as he pushed back the levers, 'not another train till daylight. My word, it is cold!'

It was intensely so. I piled some more wood on the fire and, turning up the collar of my heavy ulster, sat down at one end of the bench and leant my back against the wall. Henderson did likewise; we were neither of us inclined to speak. As a rule, whenever I have any night work to do, I am never troubled with sleepiness, but on this occasion I felt unaccountably drowsy. I soon perceived that Henderson was in the same condition.

'Are you sleepy?' I asked of him.

'Dead with it, sir,' was his answer; 'but there's no fear, I won't drop off.'

I got up and went to the window of the box. I felt certain that if I sat still any longer I should be in a sound sleep. This would never do. Already it was becoming a matter of torture to keep my eyes open. I began to pace up and down; I opened the door of the box and went out on the little platform.

'What's the matter, sir?' inquired Henderson, jumping up with a start.

'I cannot keep awake,' I said.

'Nor can I,' he answered, 'and yet I have spent nights and nights of my life in signal boxes and never was the least bit drowsy; perhaps it's the cold.'

'Perhaps it is,' I said; 'but I have been out on as freezing nights before, and—'

The man did not reply; he had sat down again; his head was nodding.

I was just about to go up to him and shake him, when it suddenly occurred to me that I might as well let him have his sleep out. I soon heard him snoring, and he presently fell forward in a heap on the floor. By dint of walking up and down, I managed to keep from dropping off myself, and in torture which I shall never be able to describe, the night wore itself away. At last, towards morning, I awoke Henderson.

'You have had a good nap,' I said; 'but never mind, I have been on guard and nothing has occurred.'

'Good God! Have I been asleep?' cried the man.

'Sound,' I answered.

'Well, I never felt anything like it,' he replied. 'Don't you find the air very close, sir?'

'No,' I said; 'it is as fresh as possible; it must be the cold.'

'I'll just go and have a look at the light at the tunnel,' said the man; 'it will rouse me.'

He went on to the little platform, whilst I bent over the fire and began to build it up. Presently he returned with a scared look on his face. I could see by the light of the oil lamp which hung on the wall that he was trembling.

'Mr Bell,' he said, 'I believe there is somebody or something down at the mouth of the tunnel now.' As he spoke he clutched me by the arm. 'Go and look,' he said; 'whoever it is, it has put out the light.'

'Put out the light?' I cried. 'Why, what's the time?'

Henderson pulled out his watch.

'Thank goodness, most of the night is gone,' he said; 'I didn't know it was so late, it is half-past five.'

'Then the local is not due for an hour yet?' I said.

'No; but who should put out the light?' cried Henderson.

I went to the door, flung it open, and looked out. The dim outline of the tunnel was just visible looming through the darkness, but the red light was out.

'What the dickens does it mean, sir?' gasped the inspector.

'I know the lamp had plenty of oil in it. Can there be anyone standing in front of it, do you think?'

We waited and watched for a few moments, but nothing stirred.

'Come along,' I said, 'let us go down together and see what it is.'

'I don't believe I can do it, sir; I really don't!'

'Nonsense,' I cried. 'I shall go down alone if you won't accompany me. Just hand me my stick, will you?'

'For God's sake, be careful, Mr Bell. Don't go down, whatever you do. I expect this is what happened before, and the poor fellows went down to see what it was and died there. There's some devilry at work, that's my belief.'

'That is as it may be,' I answered shortly; 'but we certainly shall not find out by stopping here. My business is to get to the bottom of this, and I am going to do it. That there is danger of some sort, I have very little doubt; but danger or not, I am going down.'

'If you'll be warned by me, sir, you'll just stay quietly here.'

'I must go down and see the matter out,' was my answer. 'Now listen to me, Henderson. I see that you are alarmed, and I don't wonder. Just stay quietly where you are and watch, but if I call come at once. Don't delay a single instant. Remember I am putting my life into your hands. If I call "Come", just come to me as quick as you can, for I may want help. Give me that lantern.'

He unhitched it from the wall, and taking it from him, I walked cautiously down the steps on to the line. I still felt curiously, unaccountably drowsy and heavy. I wondered at this, for the moment was such a critical one as to make almost any man wide awake.

Holding the lamp high above my head, I walked rapidly along the line. I hardly knew what I expected to find. Cautiously along the metals I made my way, peering right and left until I was close to the fatal spot where the bodies had been found. An uncontrollable shudder passed over me. The next moment, to my horror, without the slightest warning, the light I was carrying went out, leaving me in total darkness. I started back, and stumbling against one of the loose boulders reeled against the wall and nearly fell. What was the matter with me? I could hardly stand. I felt giddy and faint, and a horrible sensation of great tightness seized me across the chest. A loud ringing noise sounded in my ears. Struggling madly for breath, and with the fear of impending death upon me, I turned and tried to run from a danger I could neither understand nor grapple with. But before I had taken two steps my legs gave way from under me, and uttering a loud cry I fell insensible to the ground.

Out of an oblivion which, for all I knew, might have lasted for moments or centuries, a dawning consciousness came to me. I knew that I was lying on hard ground; that I was absolutely incapable of realising, nor had I the slightest inclination to discover, where I was. All I wanted was to lie quite still and undisturbed. Presently I opened my eyes.

Someone was bending over me and looking into my face.

'Thank God, he is not dead,' I heard in whispered tones. Then, with a flash, memory returned to me.

'What has happened?' I asked.

'You may well ask that, sir,' said the inspector gravely. 'It has been touch and go with you for the last quarter of an hour; and a near thing for me too.'

I sat up and looked around me. Daylight was just beginning to break, and I saw that we were at the bottom of the steps that led up to the signal box. My teeth were chattering with the cold and I was shivering like a man with ague.

'I am better now,' I said; 'just give me your hand.'

I took his arm, and holding the rail with the other hand staggered up into the box and sat down on the bench.

'Yes, it has been a near shave,' I said; 'and a big price to pay for solving a mystery.'

'Do you mean to say you know what it is?' asked Henderson eagerly.

'Yes,' I answered, 'I think I know now; but first tell me how long was I unconscious?'

'A good bit over half an hour, sir, I should think. As soon as I heard you call out I ran down as you told me, but before I got to you I nearly fainted. I never had such a horrible sensation in my life. I felt as weak as a baby, but I just managed to seize you by the arms and drag you along the line to the steps, and that was about all I could do.'

'Well, I owe you my life,' I said; just hand me that brandy flask, I shall be the better for some of its contents.'

I took a long pull. Just as I was laying the flask down Henderson started from my side.

'There,' he cried, 'the 6.30 is coming.' The electric bell at the instrument suddenly began to ring. 'Ought I to let her go through, sir?' he inquired.

'Certainly,' I answered. 'That is exactly what we want. Oh, she will be all right.'

'No danger to her, sir?'

'None, none; let her go through.'

He pulled the lever and the next moment the train tore through the cutting.

'Now I think it will be safe to go down again,' I said. 'I believe I shall be able to get to the bottom of this business.'

Henderson stared at me aghast.

'Do you mean that you are going down again to the tunnel?' he gasped.

'Yes,' I said; 'give me those matches. You had better come too. I don't think there will be much danger now; and there is daylight, so we can see what we are about.'

The man was very loth to obey me, but at last I managed to persuade him. We went down the line, walking slowly, and at this moment we both felt our courage revived by a broad and cheerful ray of sunshine.

'We must advance cautiously,' I said, 'and be ready to run back at a moment's notice.'

'God knows, sir, I think we are running a great risk,' panted poor Henderson; 'and if that devil or whatever else it is should happen to be about – why, daylight or no daylight—'

'Nonsense, man!' I interrupted. 'If we are careful, no harm will happen to us now. Ah! And here we are!' We had reached the spot where I had fallen. 'Just give me a match, Henderson.'

He did so, and I immediately lit the lamp. Opening the glass of the lamp, I held it close to the ground and passed it to and fro. Suddenly the flame went out.

'Don't you understand now?' I said, looking up at the inspector.

'No, I don't, sir,' he replied with a bewildered expression.

Suddenly, before I could make an explanation, we both heard shouts from the top of the cutting, and looking up I saw Bainbridge hurrying down the path. He had come in the dog-cart to fetch us.

'Here's the mystery' I cried as he rushed up to us, 'and a deadlier scheme of Dame Nature's to frighten and murder poor humanity I have never seen.'

As I spoke I lit the lamp again and held it just above a tiny fissure in the rock. It was at once extinguished.

'What is it?' said Bainbridge, panting with excitement.

'Something that nearly finished *me*,' I replied. 'Why this is a natural escape of choke damp. Carbonic acid gas – the deadliest gas imaginable, because it gives no warning of its presence, and it has no smell. It must have collected here during the hours of the night when no train was passing, and gradually rising put out the signal light. The constant rushing of the trains through the cutting all day would temporarily disperse it.'

As I made this explanation Bainbridge stood like one electrified, while a curious expression of mingled relief and horror swept over Henderson's face.

'An escape of carbonic acid gas is not an uncommon phenomenon in volcanic districts,' I continued, 'as I take this to be; but it is odd what should have started it. It has sometimes been known to follow earthquake shocks, when there is a profound disturbance of the deep strata.'

'It is strange that you should have said that,' said Bainbridge, when he could find his voice.

'What do you mean?'

'Why, that about the earthquake. Don't you remember, Henderson,' he added, turning to the inspector, 'we had felt a slight shock all over South Wales about three weeks back?'

'Then that, I think, explains it,' I said. 'It is evident that Pritchard really did climb the rocks in a frantic attempt to escape from the gas and fell back on to these boulders. The other man was cut down at once, before he had time to fly.'

'But what is to happen now?' asked Bainbridge. 'Will it go on for ever? How are we to stop it?'

'The fissure ought to be drenched with lime water, and then filled up; but all really depends on what is the size of the supply and also the depth. It is an extremely heavy gas, and would lie at the bottom of a cutting like water. I think there is more here just now than is good for us,' I added.

'But how,' continued Bainbridge, as we moved a few steps from the fatal spot, 'do you account for the interval between the first death and the second?'

'The escape must have been intermittent. If wind blew down the cutting, as probably was the case before this frost set in, it would keep the gas so diluted that its effects would not be noticed. There was enough down here this morning, before that train came through, to poison an army. Indeed, if it had not been for Henderson's promptitude, there would have been another inquest – on myself.'

I then related my own experience.

'Well, this clears Wynne, without doubt,' said Bainbridge; 'but alas for the two poor fellows who were victims! Bell, the

Lytton Vale Railway Company owes you unlimited thanks; you have doubtless saved many lives, and also the Company, for the line must have been closed if you had not made your valuable discovery. But now come home with me to breakfast. We can discuss all those matters later on.'

The Reprisal

Michael Innes

'Cellini's salt cellar?' As he sat down opposite Lord Funtington, Appleby showed surprise. 'Isn't that in Vienna?'

'You're thinking of the big one.' Funtington was impatient. 'Ours is much smaller, but the workmanship is quite as good. Cellini made it for Pope Clement VII, as he did many of his finest things. It's been in my family for quite a long time. The second earl brought it along with some other Medici treasures. You'll have heard of the Funtington Signorellis and the Funtington Piero.'

Appleby nodded. 'Certainly. I've seen them in New York.'

Lord Funtington flushed faintly. 'No doubt. We've been obliged to part, you know, with a number of our things. But we still have the salt cellar. Or we had it – until last night.'

'It's been stolen?'

Funtington hesitated. 'It's gone. The matter may be

delicate. Discretion is needed, my dear Sir John. That's why I'm uncommonly glad you have been able to come along yourself.'

'Discretion is something one has to be rather discreet about.' Appleby offered this stonily. 'May I have the facts?'

'My wife gave a party last night, and we played – well, some rather childish games. You will understand that only quite intimate friends were present. Not more than eighty guests.'

'I see. A very cosy affair. And the games?'

'The games involved scampering all over the house. And for the last one we turned off the lights. I needn't bother you with explaining it.'

Appleby nodded. 'As to that, I'm quite willing to remain in the dark for the moment. And the salt cellar?'

'There was rum punch and hot chestnuts going, and we thought it would be rather fun really to use Cellini's piece. So we stood it beside the chestnuts on a table in the grey drawing room.'

'I see.' Appleby, who had been making a note, took off his glasses and stared at Lord Funtington very hard. 'You asked some eighty people into this house, showed them a pocket-able object of enormous value, and then turned out all the lights. Am I to understand that when they came on again it was with immense surprise that you discovered the salt cellar to have vanished?'

Lord Funtington frowned. 'I'm dashed if I quite like your tone. But the thing had certainly gone.'

'What did you do?'

'Just at the moment, I didn't do anything. Or rather I consulted my wife, and we agreed that nothing could be done. There was an exalted personage present, you see, and also several distinguished foreigners. There was nothing to do but pretend not to notice, and get in touch with the police – with yourself, in fact – afterwards.'

'I suppose you've also got in touch with your insurance people?'

'Oh – of course. That goes without saying.'

Appleby nodded grimly. 'I've no doubt it does.'

'But now I'm uncommonly uneasy.' Lord Funtington hesitated once more, and rather distractedly reached for a silver cigarette box. 'Smoke? I keep on forgetting, since I don't myself. Now, what was I saying? Ah, yes. The party was only friends, as I've said. Or rather friends and relations.'

'Quite so.' Appleby had known investigations drift this way before. 'In fact, you believe that one of your own—'

The sentence remained unfinished. For a door had flung open. Lady Funtington, pale and agitated, strode into the room.

She took one glance at the two men, and appeared to divine the situation in a flash. 'Charles,' she cried, 'you must drop it. The disgrace would be unthinkable. I implore you to send that gentleman away.'

Appleby, who had stood up, smiled faintly at this note of melodrama. 'I'm afraid I can't be sent away, Lady Funtington. Your husband has called in the police, and I think he has communicated to his insurance company what is equivalent to a formal claim. Isn't that so, sir?'

Funtington, who had also risen, moved uneasily. 'My wife is right. I regret this.'

'Perhaps you do.' Appleby spoke softly. 'But I am afraid it is your duty to speak what is in your mind.'

Funtington had walked moodily to a window. When he turned round, it was to speak with a sudden unexpected savagery. 'Very well. Rupert Stride is in my mind. The name will tell you that he is my first cousin, damn him. And he's much less my friend than my wife's. He got back from some crazy wanderings in Italy a week ago, broke to the world. And his record won't bear—'

'Stop!' Lady Funtington was now looking at her husband in momentary naked fury. Appleby kept still. This sort of fracas also was sadly familiar to him. 'It's mean and horrible, Rupert—'

'No doubt, my dear, you don't relish inquiry about Rupert.' Lord Funtington gave a smile that Appleby judged extraordinarily ugly. 'But one cat is out of the bag, anyway. If your precious friend stole his own mother's diamonds, it's surely likely enough that he wouldn't stop at pocketing a bit of a mere cousin's plate.'

'But he took the diamonds when he was a mere boy!' Lady Funtington was desperate. 'And even if—'

'May I interrupt?' There was something in Appleby's voice that made the excited husband and wife fall silent at once. 'Lord Funtington, you had something to say about discretion. Well, I doubt whether it will be discreet to go on discussing the matter in this way. I have a practical measure to recommend.'

Lord Funtington produced a silk handkerchief and nervously dabbed his forehead. 'Then recommend it.'

'I can have half a dozen skilled men here in ten minutes. And I propose that they search this house.'

'Search my house!' Lord Funtington was pale with anger.

'Certainly. It is an indispensable first step on any premises from which an article of value is reported to have vanished.'

'Then search and be damned.'

'Thank you. And may I ask you both to meet me here in three hours' time?'

The salt cellar, Appleby thought, was undoubtedly a magnificent thing. It had been fitted with a glass lining to which some grains of salt still adhered. He turned it in his hands so that the jewels and enamel gleamed again. And then he looked mildly at the Funtingtons across the table. 'I'm glad it was so easy,' he said. 'To tell you the truth, sir, your dressing room was the first place I told my men to have a go at.'

Lord Funtington sprang up with a cry. He had every appearance of a man who has received a staggering shock. 'How dare you, sir! This is a monstrous impertinence ... a disgraceful trick.'

'It may certainly be the latter.' Appleby tapped the glittering salt cellar before him. 'It's easier to play tricks with – isn't it? – than a Piero or a Signorelli.' Appleby turned to Lady Funtington. 'I am afraid that this must be very painful to you. And I am also afraid that we are not yet quite at the bottom of it. Do you know what I have here?' He picked up a small object from the table and held it out before him. 'I found it wedged between the glass and the gold.'

Lady Funtington leaned forward, bewildered. 'It appears

to be a match – a sort of wax match. But an unusually small one.'

'Precisely. And it brings Mr Rupert Stride into the picture, after all. This sort of smoker's match is far smaller than anything you get in England. It comes, in fact, from Italy, where it is called *cerino*. And from Italy Mr Stride returned only last week. I don't think he gave these matches to your husband, for Lord Funtington doesn't smoke. Ah, here is what I have been waiting for.' Appleby paused as a constable entered and placed a black garment on the table before him. 'The gentleman didn't object, Joyce?'

'No, sir – said you were welcome. Amused, he seemed to be.'

'Thank you.' Appleby waited until the man had gone. 'Mr Stride's dinner jacket.' He turned the right-hand pocket inside out. 'I thought so. Salt.'

Lady Funtington stared at the tiny white pile. 'You mean that Rupert really—'

'Yes, Lady Funtington. He pocketed the salt cellar. But he did so guessing that it had been a temptation which Lord Funtington deliberately set in the way of his old weakness. Into the motive of that, we needn't enter. Mr Stride then made his way through the house under cover of darkness, and left the salt cellar where Lord Funtington would have some difficulty in accounting for its turning up. It would look, in fact, as if your husband were doing his own thieving with an eye to defrauding his insurance company.'

Appleby rose. 'Neither gentleman can be said to have behaved well. But I must say that I prefer the reprisal to the original blackguardly plot.'

The Sign of the Broken Sword

G. K. Chesterton

The thousand arms of the forest were grey, and its million fingers silver. In a sky of dark green-blue-like slate the stars were bleak and brilliant like splintered ice. All that thickly wooded and sparsely tenanted countryside was stiff with a bitter and brittle frost. The black hollows between the trunks of the trees looked like bottomless, black caverns of that Scandinavian hell, a hell of incalculable cold. Even the square stone tower of the church looked northern to the point of heathenry, as if it were some barbaric tower among the sea rocks of Iceland. It was a queer night for anyone to explore a churchyard. But, on the other hand, perhaps it was worth exploring.

It rose abruptly out of the ashen wastes of forest in a sort of hump or shoulder of green turf that looked grey in the starlight. Most of the graves were on a slant, and the path leading up to the church was as steep as a staircase. On the top of the hill, in the one flat and prominent place, was the monument for which the place was famous. It contrasted strangely with the featureless graves all round, for it was the work of one of the greatest sculptors of modern Europe; and yet his fame was at once forgotten in the fame of the man whose image he had made. It showed, by touches of the small silver pencil of starlight, the massive metal figure of a soldier recumbent, the strong hands sealed in an everlasting worship, the great head pillowed upon a gun. The venerable face was bearded, or rather whiskered, in the old, heavy Colonel Newcome fashion. The uniform, though suggested with the few strokes of simplicity, was that of modern war. By his right side lay a sword, of which the tip was broken off; on the left side lay a Bible. On glowing summer afternoons wagonettes came full of Americans and cultured suburbans to see the sepulchre; but even then they felt the vast forest land with its one dumpy dome of churchyard and church as a place oddly dumb and neglected. In this freezing darkness of mid-winter one would think he might be left alone with the stars. Nevertheless, in the stillness of those stiff woods a wooden gate creaked, and two dim figures dressed in black climbed up the little path to the tomb.

So faint was that frigid starlight that nothing could have been traced about them except that while they both wore black, one man was enormously big, and the other (perhaps by contrast) almost startlingly small. They went up to the great graven tomb of the historic warrior, and stood for a few minutes staring at it. There was no human, perhaps no living, thing for a wide circle; and a morbid fancy might well have wondered if they were human themselves. In any case, the beginning of their conversation might have seemed strange. After the first silence the small man said to the other:

'Where does a wise man hide a pebble?'

And the tall man answered in a low voice: 'On the beach.'

The small man nodded, and after a short silence said: 'Where does a wise man hide a leaf?'

And the other answered: 'In the forest.'

There was another stillness, and then the tall man resumed: 'Do you mean that when a wise man has to hide a real diamond he has been known to hide it among sham ones?'

'No, no,' said the little man with a laugh, 'we will let bygones be bygones.'

He stamped his cold feet for a second or two, and then said: 'I'm not thinking of that at all, but of something else; something rather peculiar. Just strike a match, will you?'

The big man fumbled in his pocket, and soon a scratch and a flare painted gold the whole flat side of the monument. On it was cut in black letters the well-known words which so many Americans had reverently read: 'Sacred to the Memory of General Sir Arthur St. Clare, Hero and Martyr, who Always Vanquished his Enemies and Always Spared Them, and Was Treacherously Slain by Them At Last. May God in Whom he Trusted both Reward and Revenge him.'

The match burnt the big man's fingers, blackened, and dropped. He was about to strike another, but his small companion stopped him. 'That's all right, Flambeau, old man;

I saw what I wanted. Or, rather, I didn't see what I didn't want. And now we must walk a mile and a half along the road to the next inn, and I will try to tell you all about it. For Heaven knows a man should have a fire and ale when he dares tell such a story.'

They descended the precipitous path, they relatched the rusty gate, and set off at a stamping, ringing walk down the frozen forest road. They had gone a full quarter of a mile before the smaller man spoke again. He said: 'Yes; the wise man hides a pebble on the beach. But what does he do if there is no beach? Do you know anything of that great St. Clare trouble?'

'I know nothing about English generals, Father Brown,' answered the large man, laughing, 'though a little about English policemen. I only know that you have dragged me a precious long dance to all the shrines of this fellow, whoever he is. One would think he got buried in six different places. I've seen a memorial to General St. Clare in Westminster Abbey. I've seen a ramping equestrian statue of General St. Clare on the Embankment. I've seen a medallion of St. Clare in the street he was born in, and another in the street he lived in; and now you drag me after dark to his coffin in the village churchyard. I am beginning to be a bit tired of his magnificent personality, especially as I don't in the least know who he was. What are you hunting for in all these crypts and effigies?'

'I am only looking for one word,' said Father Brown. 'A word that isn't there.'

'Well,' asked Flambeau; 'are you going to tell me anything about it?'

'I must divide it into two parts,' remarked the priest. 'First there is what everybody knows; and then there is what I know. Now, what everybody knows is short and plain enough. It is also entirely wrong.'

'Right you are,' said the big man called Flambeau cheerfully. 'Let's begin at the wrong end. Let's begin with what everybody knows, which isn't true.'

'If not wholly untrue, it is at least very inadequate,' continued Brown; 'for in point of fact, all that the public knows amounts precisely to this: The public knows that Arthur St. Clare was a great and successful English general. It knows that after splendid yet careful campaigns both in India and Africa he was in command against Brazil when the great Brazilian patriot Olivier issued his ultimatum. It knows that on that occasion St. Clare with a very small force attacked Olivier with a very large one, and was captured after heroic resistance. And it knows that after his capture, and to the abhorrence of the civilised world, St. Clare was hanged on the nearest tree. He was found swinging there after the Brazilians had retired, with his broken sword hung round his neck.'

'And that popular story is untrue?' suggested Flambeau.

'No,' said his friend quietly, 'that story is quite true, so far as it goes.'

'Well, I think it goes far enough!' said Flambeau; 'but if the popular story is true, what is the mystery?'

They had passed many hundreds of grey and ghostly trees before the little priest answered. Then he bit his finger reflectively and said: 'Why, the mystery is a mystery of psychology. Or, rather, it is a mystery of two psychologies. In that Brazilian business two of the most famous men of modern history acted flat against their characters. Mind you, Olivier and St. Clare were both heroes – the old thing, and no mistake; it was like the fight between Hector and Achilles. Now, what would you say to an affair in which Achilles was timid and Hector was treacherous?'

'Go on,' said the large man impatiently as the other bit his finger again.

'Sir Arthur St. Clare was a soldier of the old religious type – the type that saved us during the Mutiny,' continued Brown. 'He was always more for duty than for dash; and with all his personal courage was decidedly a prudent commander, particularly indignant at any needless waste of soldiers. Yet in this last battle he attempted something that a baby could see was absurd. One need not be a strategist to see it was as wild as wind; just as one need not be a strategist to keep out of the way of a motor-bus. Well, that is the first mystery; what had become of the English general's head? The second riddle is, what had become of the Brazilian general's heart? President Olivier might be called a visionary or a nuisance; but even his enemies admitted that he was magnanimous to the point of knight errantry. Almost every other prisoner he had ever captured had been set free or even loaded with benefits. Men who had really wronged him came away touched by his simplicity and sweetness. Why the deuce should he diabolically revenge himself only once in his life; and that for the one particular blow that could not have hurt him? Well, there you have it. One of the wisest men in the world acted like an idiot for no reason. One of the best men in the world acted like a fiend for no reason. That's the long and the short of it; and I leave it to you, my boy.'

'No, you don't,' said the other with a snort. 'I leave it to you; and you jolly well tell me all about it.'

'Well,' resumed Father Brown, 'it's not fair to say that the public impression is just what I've said, without adding that two things have happened since. I can't say they threw a new light; for nobody can make sense of them. But they threw a new kind of darkness; they threw the darkness in new directions. The first was this. The family physician of the St. Clares quarrelled with that family, and began publishing a violent series of articles, in which he said that the late general was a religious maniac; but as far as the tale went, this seemed to mean little more than a religious man.

'Anyhow, the story fizzled out. Everyone knew, of course, that St. Clare had some of the eccentricities of puritan piety. The second incident was much more arresting. In the luckless and unsupported regiment which made that rash attempt at the Black River there was a certain Captain Keith, who was at that time engaged to St. Clare's daughter, and who afterwards married her. He was one of those who were captured by Olivier, and, like all the rest except the general, appears to have been bounteously treated and promptly set free. Some twenty years afterwards this man, then Lieutenant-Colonel Keith, published a sort of autobiography called *A British Officer in Burmah and Brazil*. In the place where the reader looks eagerly for some account of the mystery of St. Clare's disaster may be found the following words: "Everywhere else in this book I have narrated things exactly as they occurred, holding as I do the old-fashioned opinion that the glory of England is old enough to take care of itself. The exception I shall make is in this matter of the defeat by the Black River; and my reasons, though private, are honourable and compelling. I will, however, add this in justice to the memories of two distinguished men. General St. Clare has been accused of incapacity on this occasion; I can at least testify that this action, properly understood, was one of the most brilliant and sagacious of his life. President Olivier by similar report is charged with savage injustice. I think it due to the honour of an enemy to say that he acted on this occasion with even more than his characteristic good feeling. To put the matter popularly, I can assure my countrymen that St. Clare was by no means such a fool nor Olivier such a brute as he looked. This is all I have to say; nor shall any earthly consideration induce me to add a word to it."'

A large frozen moon like a lustrous snowball began to show through the tangle of twigs in front of them, and by its light the narrator had been able to refresh his memory of Captain Keith's text from a scrap of printed paper. As he folded it up and put it back in his pocket Flambeau threw up his hand with a French gesture.

'Wait a bit, wait a bit,' he cried excitedly. 'I believe I can guess it at the first go.'

He strode on, breathing hard, his black head and bull neck forward, like a man winning a walking race. The little priest, amused and interested, had some trouble in trotting beside him. Just before them the trees fell back a little to left and right, and the road swept downwards across a clear, moonlit valley, till it dived again like a rabbit into the wall of another wood. The entrance to the farther forest looked small and round, like the black hole of a remote railway tunnel. But it was within some hundred yards, and gaped like a cavern before Flambeau spoke again.

'I've got it,' he cried at last, slapping his thigh with his great hand. 'Four minutes' thinking, and I can tell your whole story myself.'

'All right,' assented his friend. 'You tell it.'

Flambeau lifted his head, but lowered his voice. 'General Sir Arthur St. Clare,' he said, 'came of a family in which madness was hereditary; and his whole aim was to keep this from his daughter, and even, if possible, from his future son-in-law. Rightly or wrongly, he thought the final collapse was close, and resolved on suicide. Yet ordinary suicide would blazon the very idea he dreaded. As the campaign approached the clouds came thicker on his brain; and at last in a mad moment he sacrificed his public duty to his private. He rushed rashly into battle, hoping to fall by the first shot. When he found that he had only attained capture and discredit, the sealed bomb in his brain burst, and he broke his own sword and hanged himself.'

He stared firmly at the grey facade of forest in front of him, with the one black gap in it, like the mouth of the grave, into which their path plunged. Perhaps something menacing in the road thus suddenly swallowed reinforced his vivid vision of the tragedy, for he shuddered.

'A horrid story,' he said.

'A horrid story,' repeated the priest with bent head. 'But not the real story.'

Then he threw back his head with a sort of despair and cried: 'Oh, I wish it had been.'

The tall Flambeau faced round and stared at him.

'Yours is a clean story,' cried Father Brown, deeply moved. 'A sweet, pure, honest story, as open and white as that moon. Madness and despair are innocent enough. There are worse things, Flambeau.'

Flambeau looked up wildly at the moon thus invoked; and from where he stood one black tree-bough curved across it exactly like a devil's horn.

'Father – father,' cried Flambeau with the French gesture and stepping yet more rapidly forward, 'do you mean it was worse than that?'

'Worse than that,' said Paul like a grave echo. And they plunged into the black cloister of the woodland, which ran by them in a dim tapestry of trunks, like one of the dark corridors in a dream.

They were soon in the most secret entrails of the wood, and felt close about them foliage that they could not see, when the priest said again:

'Where does a wise man hide a leaf? In the forest. But what does he do if there is no forest?'

'Well, well,' cried Flambeau irritably, 'what does he do?'

'He grows a forest to hide it in,' said the priest in an obscure voice. 'A fearful sin.'

'Look here,' cried his friend impatiently, for the dark wood and the dark saying got a little on his nerves; 'will you tell me this story or not? What other evidence is there to go on?'

'There are three more bits of evidence,' said the other, 'that I have dug up in holes and corners; and I will give them in logical rather than chronological order. First of all, of course, our authority for the issue and event of the battle is in Olivier's own dispatches, which are lucid enough. He was entrenched with two or three regiments on the heights that swept down to the Black River, on the other side of which was lower and more marshy ground. Beyond this again was gently rising country, on which was the first English outpost, supported by others which lay, however, considerably in its rear. The British forces as a whole were greatly superior in numbers; but this particular regiment was just far enough from its base to make Olivier consider the project of crossing the river to cut it off. By sunset, however, he had decided to retain his own position, which was a specially strong one. At daybreak next morning he was thunderstruck to see that this stray handful of English, entirely unsupported from their rear, had flung themselves across the river, half by a bridge to the right, and the other half by a ford higher up, and were massed upon the marshy bank below him.

'That they should attempt an attack with such numbers against such a position was incredible enough; but Olivier noticed something yet more extraordinary. For instead of attempting to seize more solid ground, this mad regiment, having put the river in its rear by one wild charge, did nothing more, but stuck there in the mire like flies in treacle. Needless to say, the Brazilians blew great gaps in them with artillery, which they could only return with spirited but lessening rifle fire. Yet they never broke; and Olivier's curt account ends with a strong tribute of admiration for the mystic valour of these imbeciles. "Our line then advanced finally," writes Olivier, "and drove them into the river; we captured General St. Clare himself and several other officers. The colonel and the major had both fallen in the battle. I cannot resist saying that few finer sights can have been seen in history than the last stand of this extraordinary regiment; wounded officers picking up the rifles of dead soldiers, and the general himself facing us on horseback bareheaded and with a broken sword." On what happened to the general afterwards Olivier is as silent as Captain Keith.'

'Well,' grunted Flambeau, 'get on to the next bit of evidence.'

'The next evidence,' said Father Brown, 'took some time to find, but it will not take long to tell. I found at last in an almshouse down in the Lincolnshire Fens an old soldier who not only was wounded at the Black River, but had actually knelt beside the colonel of the regiment when he died. This latter was a certain Colonel Clancy, a big bull of an Irishman; and it would seem that he died almost as much of rage as of bullets. He, at any rate, was not responsible for that ridiculous raid; it must have been imposed on him by the general. His last edifying words, according to my informant, were these: "And there goes the damned old donkey with the end of his sword knocked off. I wish it was his head." You will remark that everyone seems to have noticed this detail about the broken sword blade, though most people regard it somewhat more reverently than did the late Colonel Clancy. And now for the third fragment.'

Their path through the woodland began to go upward, and the speaker paused a little for breath before he went on. Then he continued in the same business-like tone:

'Only a month or two ago a certain Brazilian official died in England, having quarrelled with Olivier and left his country. He was a well-known figure both here and on the Continent, a Spaniard named Espado; I knew him myself, a yellow-faced old dandy, with a hooked nose. For various private reasons I had permission to see the documents he had left; he was a Catholic, of course, and I had been with him towards the end. There was nothing of his that lit up any corner of the black St. Clare business, except five or six common exercise books filled with the diary of some English soldier. I can only suppose that it was found by the Brazilians on one of those that fell. Anyhow, it stopped abruptly the night before the battle.

'But the account of that last day in the poor fellow's life was certainly worth reading. I have it on me; but it's too dark to read it here, and I will give you a résumé. The first part of that entry is full of jokes, evidently flung about among the men, about somebody called the Vulture. It does not seem as if this person, whoever he was, was one of themselves, nor even an Englishman; neither is he exactly spoken of as one of the enemy. It sounds rather as if he were some local go-between and non-combatant; perhaps a guide or a journalist. He has been closeted with old Colonel Clancy; but is more often seen talking to the major. Indeed, the major is somewhat prominent in this soldier's narrative; a lean, dark-haired man, apparently, of the name of Murray – a north of Ireland man and a Puritan. There are continual jests about the contrast between this Ulsterman's austerity and the conviviality of Colonel Clancy. There is also some joke about the Vulture wearing bright-coloured clothes.

'But all these levities are scattered by what may well be called the note of a bugle. Behind the English camp and almost parallel to the river ran one of the few great roads of that district. Westward the road curved round towards the river, which it crossed by the bridge before mentioned. To the east the road swept backwards into the wilds, and some two miles along it was the next English outpost. From this direction there came along the road that evening a glitter and clatter of light cavalry, in which even the simple diarist could recognise with astonishment the general with his staff. He rode the great white horse which you have seen so often in illustrated papers and Academy pictures; and you may be sure that the salute they gave him was not merely ceremonial. He, at least, wasted no time on ceremony, but, springing from the saddle immediately, mixed with the group of officers, and fell into emphatic though confidential speech. What struck our friend the diarist most was his special disposition to discuss matters with Major Murray; but, indeed, such a selection, so long as it was not marked, was in no way unnatural. The two men were made for sympathy; they were men who "read their Bibles"; they were both the old Evangelical type of officer. However this may be, it is certain that when the general mounted again he was still talking earnestly to Murray; and that as he walked his horse slowly down the road towards the river, the tall Ulsterman still walked by his bridle rein in earnest debate. The soldiers watched the two until they vanished behind a clump of trees where the road turned towards the river. The colonel had gone back to his tent, and the men to their pickets; the man with the diary lingered for another four minutes, and saw a marvellous sight.

'The great white horse which had marched slowly down the road, as it had marched in so many processions, flew back, galloping up the road towards them as if it were mad to win a race. At first they thought it had run away with the man on its back; but they soon saw that the general, a fine rider, was himself urging it to full speed. Horse and man swept up to them like a whirlwind; and then, reining up the reeling charger, the general turned on them a face like flame, and called for the colonel like the trumpet that wakes the dead.

'I conceive that all the earthquake events of that catastrophe tumbled on top of each other rather like lumber in the minds of men such as our friend with the diary. With the dazed excitement of a dream, they found themselves falling – literally falling – into their ranks, and learned that an attack was to be led at once across the river. The general and the major, it was said, had found out something at the bridge, and there was only just time to strike for life. The major had gone back at once to call up the reserve along the road behind; it was doubtful if even with that prompt appeal help could reach them in time. But they must pass the stream that night, and seize the heights by morning. It is with the very stir and throb of that romantic nocturnal march that the diary suddenly ends.'

Father Brown had mounted ahead; for the woodland path grew smaller, steeper, and more twisted, till they felt as if they were ascending a winding staircase. The priest's voice came from above out of the darkness.

'There was one other little and enormous thing. When the general urged them to their chivalric charge he half drew his sword from the scabbard; and then, as if ashamed of such melodrama, thrust it back again. The sword again, you see.'

A half-light broke through the network of boughs above them, flinging the ghost of a net about their feet; for they were mounting again to the faint luminosity of the naked night. Flambeau felt truth all round him as an atmosphere, but not as an idea. He answered with bewildered brain: 'Well, what's the matter with the sword? Officers generally have swords, don't they?'

'They are not often mentioned in modern war,' said the other dispassionately; 'but in this affair one falls over the blessed sword everywhere.'

'Well, what is there in that?' growled Flambeau; 'it was a twopence coloured sort of incident; the old man's blade breaking in his last battle. Anyone might bet the papers would get hold of it, as they have. On all these tombs and things it's shown broken at the point. I hope you haven't dragged me through this Polar expedition merely because two men with an eye for a picture saw St. Clare's broken sword.'

'No,' cried Father Brown, with a sharp voice like a pistol shot; 'but who saw his unbroken sword?'

'What do you mean?' cried the other, and stood still under the stars. They had come abruptly out of the grey gates of the wood.

'I say, who saw his unbroken sword?' repeated Father Brown obstinately. 'Not the writer of the diary, anyhow; the general sheathed it in time.'

Flambeau looked about him in the moonlight, as a man struck blind might look in the sun; and his friend went on, for the first time with eagerness:

'Flambeau,' he cried, 'I cannot prove it, even after hunting through the tombs. But I am sure of it. Let me add just one more tiny fact that tips the whole thing over. The colonel, by a strange chance, was one of the first struck by a bullet. He was struck long before the troops came to close quarters. But he saw St. Clare's sword broken. Why was it broken? How was it broken? My friend, it was broken before the battle.'

'Oh!' said his friend, with a sort of forlorn jocularity; 'and pray where is the other piece?'

'I can tell you,' said the priest promptly. 'In the north-east corner of the cemetery of the Protestant Cathedral at Belfast.'

'Indeed?' inquired the other. 'Have you looked for it?'

'I couldn't,' replied Brown, with frank regret. 'There's a great marble monument on top of it; a monument to the heroic Major Murray, who fell fighting gloriously at the famous Battle of the Black River.'

Flambeau seemed suddenly galvanised into existence. 'You mean,' he cried hoarsely, 'that General St. Clare hated Murray, and murdered him on the field of battle because—'

'You are still full of good and pure thoughts,' said the other. 'It was worse than that.'

'Well,' said the large man, 'my stock of evil imagination is used up.'

The priest seemed really doubtful where to begin, and at last he said again:

'Where would a wise man hide a leaf? In the forest.'

The other did not answer.

'If there were no forest, he would make a forest. And if he wished to hide a dead leaf, he would make a dead forest.'

There was still no reply, and the priest added still more mildly and quietly:

'And if a man had to hide a dead body, he would make a field of dead bodies to hide it in.'

Flambeau began to stamp forward with an intolerance of delay in time or space; but Father Brown went on as if he were continuing the last sentence:

'Sir Arthur St. Clare, as I have already said, was a man who read his Bible. That was what was the matter with him. When will people understand that it is useless for a man to read his Bible unless he also reads everybody else's Bible? A printer reads a Bible for misprints. A Mormon reads his Bible, and finds polygamy; a Christian Scientist reads his, and finds we have no arms and legs. St. Clare was an old Anglo-Indian Protestant soldier. Now, just think what that might mean; and, for Heaven's sake, don't cant about it. It might mean a man physically formidable living under a tropic sun in an Oriental society, and soaking himself without sense or guidance in an Oriental Book. Of course, he read the Old Testament rather than the New. Of course, he found in the Old Testament anything that he wanted – lust, tyranny, treason. Oh, I dare say he was honest, as you call it. But what is the good of a man being honest in his worship of dishonesty?

'In each of the hot and secret countries to which the man went he kept a harem, he tortured witnesses, he amassed shameful gold; but certainly he would have said with steady eyes that he did it to the glory of the Lord. My own theology is sufficiently expressed by asking which Lord? Anyhow, there is this about such evil, that it opens door after door in hell, and always into smaller and smaller chambers. This is the real case against crime, that a man does not become wilder and wilder, but only meaner and meaner. St. Clare was soon suffocated by difficulties of bribery and blackmail; and needed more and more cash. And by the time of the Battle of the Black River he had fallen from world to world to that place which Dante makes the lowest floor of the universe.'

'What do you mean?' asked his friend again.

'I mean that,' retorted the cleric, and suddenly pointed at a puddle sealed with ice that shone in the moon. 'Do you remember whom Dante put in the last circle of ice?'

'The traitors,' said Flambeau, and shuddered. As he looked around at the inhuman landscape of trees, with taunting and almost obscene outlines, he could almost fancy he was Dante, and the priest with the rivulet of a voice was, indeed, a Virgil leading him through a land of eternal sins.

The voice went on: 'Olivier, as you know, was quixotic, and would not permit a secret service and spies. The thing, however, was done, like many other things, behind his back. It was managed by my old friend Espado; he was the bright-clad fop, whose hook nose got him called the Vulture. Posing as a sort of philanthropist at the front, he felt his way through the English Army, and at last got his fingers on its one corrupt man – please God! – and that man at the top. St. Clare was in foul need of money, and mountains of it. The discredited family doctor was threatening those extraordinary exposures that afterwards began and were broken off; tales of monstrous and prehistoric things in Park Lane; things done by an English Evangelist that smelt like human sacrifice and hordes of slaves. Money was wanted, too, for his daughter's dowry; for to him the fame of wealth was as sweet as wealth itself. He snapped the last thread, whispered the word to Brazil, and wealth poured in from the enemies of England. But another man had talked to Espado the Vulture as well as he. Somehow the dark, grim young major from Ulster had guessed the hideous truth; and when they walked slowly together down that road towards the bridge Murray was telling the general that he must resign instantly, or be court-martialled and shot. The general temporised with him till they came to the fringe of tropic trees by the bridge; and there by the singing river and the sunlit palms (for I can see the picture) the general drew his sabre and plunged it through the body of the major.'

The wintry road curved over a ridge in cutting frost, with cruel black shapes of bush and thicket; but Flambeau fancied that he saw beyond it faintly the edge of an aureole that was not starlight and moonlight, but some fire such as is made by men. He watched it as the tale drew to its close.

'St. Clare was a hell-hound, but he was a hound of breed. Never, I'll swear, was he so lucid and so strong as when poor Murray lay a cold lump at his feet. Never in all his triumphs, as Captain Keith said truly, was the great man so great as he was in this last world-despised defeat. He looked coolly at his weapon to wipe off the blood; he saw the point he had planted between his victim's shoulders had broken off in the body. He saw quite calmly, as through a club windowpane, all that must follow. He saw that men must find the unaccountable corpse; must extract the unaccountable sword-point; must notice the unaccountable broken sword – or absence of sword. He had killed, but not silenced. But his imperious intellect rose against the facer; there was one way yet. He could make the corpse less unaccountable. He could create a hill of corpses to cover this one. In twenty minutes eight hundred English soldiers were marching down to their death.'

The warmer glow behind the black winter wood grew richer and brighter, and Flambeau strode on to reach it. Father Brown also quickened his stride; but he seemed merely absorbed in his tale.

'Such was the valour of that English thousand, and such the genius of their commander, that if they had at once attacked the hill, even their mad march might have met some luck. But the evil mind that played with them like pawns had other aims and reasons. They must remain in the marshes by the bridge at least till British corpses should be a common sight there. Then for the last grand scene; the silver-haired soldier-saint would give up his shattered sword to save further slaughter. Oh, it was well organised for an impromptu. But I think (I cannot prove), I think that it was while they stuck there in the bloody mire that someone doubted – and someone guessed.'

He was mute a moment, and then said: 'There is a voice from nowhere that tells me the man who guessed was the lover ... the man to wed the old man's child.'

'But what about Olivier and the hanging?' asked Flambeau.

'Olivier, partly from chivalry, partly from policy, seldom encumbered his march with captives,' explained the narrator. 'He released everybody in most cases. He released everybody in this case.'

'Everybody but the general,' said the tall man.

'Everybody,' said the priest.

Flambeau knit his black brows. 'I don't grasp it all yet,' he said.

'There is another picture, Flambeau,' said Brown in his

more mystical undertone. 'I can't prove it; but I can do more – I can see it. There is a camp breaking up on the bare, torrid hills at morning, and Brazilian uniforms massed in blocks and columns to march. There is the red shirt and long black beard of Olivier, which blows as he stands, his broad-brimmed hat in his hand. He is saying farewell to the great enemy he is setting free – the simple, snow-headed English veteran, who thanks him in the name of his men. The English remnant stand behind at attention; beside them are stores and vehicles for the retreat. The drums roll; the Brazilians are moving; the English are still like statues. So they abide till the last hum and flash of the enemy have faded from the tropic horizon. Then they alter their postures all at once, like dead men coming to life; they turn their fifty faces upon the general – faces not to be forgotten.'

Flambeau gave a great jump. 'Ah,' he cried, 'you don't mean—'

'Yes,' said Father Brown in a deep, moving voice. 'It was an English hand that put the rope round St. Clare's neck; I believe the hand that put the ring on his daughter's finger. They were English hands that dragged him up to the tree of shame; the hands of men that had adored him and followed him to victory. And they were English souls (God pardon and endure us all!) who stared at him swinging in that foreign sun on the green gallows of palm, and prayed in their hatred that he might drop off it into hell.'

As the two topped the ridge there burst on them the strong scarlet light of a red-curtained English inn. It stood sideways in the road, as if standing aside in the amplitude of hospitality. Its three doors stood open with invitation; and even where they stood they could hear the hum and laughter of humanity happy for a night.

'I need not tell you more,' said Father Brown. 'They tried him in the wilderness and destroyed him; and then, for the honour of England and of his daughter, they took an oath to seal up for ever the story of the traitor's purse and the assassin's sword blade. Perhaps – Heaven help them – they tried to forget it. Let us try to forget it, anyhow; here is our inn.'

'With all my heart,' said Flambeau, and was just striding into the bright, noisy bar when he stepped back and almost fell on the road.

'Look there, in the devil's name!' he cried, and pointed rigidly at the square wooden sign that overhung the road. It showed dimly the crude shape of a sabre hilt and a shortened blade; and was inscribed in false archaic lettering, 'The Sign of the Broken Sword'.

'Were you not prepared?' asked Father Brown gently. 'He is the god of this country; half the inns and parks and streets are named after him and his story.'

'I thought we had done with the leper,' cried Flambeau, and spat on the road.

'You will never have done with him in England,' said the priest, looking down, 'while brass is strong and stone abides. His marble statues will erect the souls of proud, innocent boys for centuries, his village tomb will smell of loyalty as of lilies. Millions who never knew him shall love him like a father – this man whom the last few that knew him dealt with like dung. He shall be a saint; and the truth shall never be told of him, because I have made up my mind at last. There is so much good and evil in breaking secrets, that I put my conduct to a test. All these newspapers will perish; the anti-Brazil boom is already over; Olivier is already honoured everywhere. But I told myself that if anywhere, by name, in metal or marble that will endure like the pyramids, Colonel Clancy, or Captain Keith, or President Olivier, or any innocent man was wrongly blamed, then I would speak. If it were only that St. Clare was wrongly praised, I would be silent. And I will.'

They plunged into the red-curtained tavern, which was not only cosy, but even luxurious inside. On a table stood a silver model of the tomb of St. Clare, the silver head bowed, the silver sword broken. On the walls were coloured photographs of the same scene, and of the system of wagonettes that took tourists to see it. They sat down on the comfortable padded benches.

'Come, it's cold,' cried Father Brown; 'let's have some wine or beer.'

'Or brandy,' said Flambeau.

Off the Tiles

Ianthe Jerrold

November gloom had descended on London when, at 1752 hours (5.52 pm on unofficial clocks), a telephone call was received at the Pine Road, Chelsea, police station. The speaker, a Mrs Flitcroft, of 33 Chain Street, said that her next-door neighbour, a Miss Lillah Keer, had been killed by falling from the roof of her house on to the pavement. Inspector James Quy ordered an ambulance, and went at once by car to Chain Street, accompanied by PC Baker.

Quy knew Chain Street well, for he had recently investigated a burglary there. The houses were terrace-built, old-fashioned, stucco-faced, single-fronted, consisting each of three storeys above the ground floor, and a basement below, with a narrow area railed off from the pavement, and several steps up to the front door. The roofs, he remembered, were of the mansard type, with small windows opening upon a leaded gutter and a low parapet. It would not be possible to fall accidentally out of such a window, and Quy therefore anticipated a case of suicide, for ladies do not usually walk about on roofs unless their nerves are disturbed and their intentions self-destructive. However, when he arrived in Chain Street, he found that the matter was by no means so simple.

Light streamed from the open front doors of Numbers 33 and 31, and there was a little knot of people gathered on the pavement at a spot almost exactly between the two houses. Looking up, Quy saw that, as he had supposed, a continuous parapet ran outside the mansard windows all along the terrace. He had time to note also that the mansard window in Number 31 was of the casement type, that in Number 33 of the sash, before three people started speaking to him all at once as he got out of his car. One was a pale young man with dark hair and a nervous blink behind horn-rimmed glasses, who said: 'Oh, Officer! If only I hadn't had my wireless on! If only I'd heard!' The second was a pale, grey-haired woman who looked pinched and wretched in a thin silk blouse, and had obviously been weeping, who said tremulously: 'I'm Mrs Flitcroft – I rang you up!' And the third was a tall, square-faced woman in a red coat and a necklace of huge amber beads, who cried passionately: 'I'm her sister – I've only just got back! It *couldn't* have been an accident! I've done it myself often!'

Quy paused to ask:

'Done what?'

'Why, walked along the roof-gutter!' she replied. 'It's nothing, it's perfectly safe, whatever that old fool says! And so have other people done it – you couldn't fall off if you tried!'

She then glared with hatred at the other woman, and broke into tears, and Inspector Quy heard the word 'murder' as she turned aside.

'All right,' said Quy. 'Just stand by, will you? I'll want you later.' And the onlookers falling back before his uniform, he found himself facing a very old gentleman over the prone body of a middle-aged woman with a fur coat spread over her. A stethoscope dangled from the old gentleman's neck.

'The poor lady's dead,' said the old gentleman crossly.

'Did she say anything, Doctor?'

'Not to me! Broken skull, spinal injuries, and goodness knows what else! Crawling about on roofs at her age!'

'There's a lady here says it's quite safe and she's often done it herself.'

'Imagine it! Women of fifty and sixty crawling about roofs to pay calls by the attic windows, like cats! Never think of their blood pressure, I suppose – never heard of vertigo! Heart failure, stiff joints, poor eyesight – couldn't happen to *them*, oh no! That's what's the matter with the world today, if you ask me! Nobody knows his place! Insane, there's no other word for it ... Well, there's nothing more I can do, so I'll be getting home, Inspector, I'm freezing! You know where to find me if you want me.' And the very old gentleman went off, stiffly but energetically, swinging his stethoscope.

Inspector Quy turned back the fur coat that covered the body of Miss Lillah Keer, who was a slightly smaller, slightly younger, version of her sister Miss Rachel, now weeping noisily against the area railings. It was not, however, at the poor lady's face that Quy first looked, but at her hands. They were grimy, as might be expected. In a broken fingernail on the left hand, a small piece of very dirty cotton waste was caught. Inspector Quy took it out and carefully examined it. It had a faint scent reminiscent of turpentine. There were traces of the same kind of cotton fluff under the other nails on the left hand. Inspector Quy saw the other Miss Keer standing beside him, and asked:

'Was your sister left-handed?'

'No!' she replied fiercely. And she wasn't a clumsy ass, either! And I tell you, it *wasn't* an accident! It was murder, and I know who did it!'

'You can tell me about that later – in fact, you'll have to!' said Quy. 'But meanwhile, your sister was right-handed?'

'She could use both her hands pretty well, like most artists,' said Miss Keer, more quietly.

'Oh, your sister was an artist?'

'She painted with her right hand, of course, but she often used her left to mix her colours, or to clean her palette.'

'With turpentine, I suppose?'

'Yes, or some patent stuff artists' colourmen sell.'

'And cotton waste?'

'Or household rags.'

'I see,' said Inspector Quy. Further investigations were interrupted by the arrival of the ambulance and the police surgeon. When they had departed again, and the small crowd of onlookers had lingeringly dispersed, Quy took down the evidence and particulars of the inmates of the two houses. Mrs Flitcroft of Number 33, a widow living with her son and daughter; Peter Crangley, aged twenty-four, nephew to

Mrs Flitcroft, a civil servant, who occupied the top floor of his aunt's house; and Miss Rachel Keer, elder sister of the deceased, a schoolteacher, who had shared Number 31 for many years with the dead lady.

'Whose fur coat is this?' asked Quy. They were standing in the ground-floor room of Miss Keer's house.

'Mine,' said Mrs Flitcroft. 'I took it off and put it over her . . .'

As Quy passed it to her, there was a distinct jingle in one of its pockets. Mrs Flitcroft heard it, and a sudden look of fright came to her careworn face.

'What is it?' asked Quy.

She said with difficulty and distress:

'The keys! Oh, they were in my coat pocket all the time!'

From one of the pockets of the fur coat she brought out with a shaking hand a small bunch of keys. 'But I'm *sure* I *felt* in my pockets!' she exclaimed, with tears.

'You *knew* they were there!' cried Miss Rachel Keer, her face distorted with hatred. 'There, Inspector! I told you! This woman murdered my sister! It was just an excuse to get Lillah out on the roof and push her over the parapet! I tell you, Inspector, this woman hated my sister; she's hated her ever since—'

'I didn't!' protested Mrs Flitcroft tearfully. 'I don't hate people! I'm not like you!'

'No, you're the sly kind that never says what she thinks, but waits for an opportunity to hurt – stab in the back – push off the roof! You know you've hated Lillah ever since she started taking an interest in Peter—'

'Me?' exclaimed young Mr Crangley with dramatic surprise.

'One thing at a time, please!' said Quy, as PC Baker, sitting at the dining table with his helmet on a chair beside him, began to look worried over his short-hand notes. 'Tell me about the keys. What happened?'

It appeared that Mrs Flitcroft, on returning to her house at about half-past five, had discovered that her keys were not in her handbag – 'though I can't *think* why not! I *never* keep them anywhere else! I thought they weren't in my pockets, either! I'm sure I felt in my pockets!' – and had rung her bell and banged on her knocker to attract the attention of her nephew, whose light she could see in the top window. She had also called to him, but he had not heard her.

'It was the damned wireless!' groaned the young man.

Mrs Flitcroft's son and daughter were going straight from their businesses to a theatre, and would not be back until late; and since her nephew lived his own domestic life in his top flat and would not miss her, she was faced with the alternatives of staying out of her house until ten o'clock, or swallowing her pride and going next door for help. She admitted that she had had a serious quarrel with Miss Lillah Keer a month or two ago, over – over Peter, she said, glancing at that young man. She had thought it very wrong of Miss Keer to encourage her nephew in his desire to be a painter.

'Oh, you're a painter, too?' said Quy. 'I thought you said you were a civil servant?'

'I work in the Post Office because I have to earn my living, unfortunately.'

'That's a misfortune that occurs to a good many people,'

said Quy, smiling. 'You're not at work today?'

'No, I—'

'Exactly!' said Mrs Flitcroft with tremulous indignation. 'He doesn't stick to his work! And there she was, poor Miss Keer, telling him he had talent for art, giving him free lessons and quite turning his head! He *has* to earn his living, and his mother asked me to look after him; and even if he *could* paint, there's no living in art!'

There was no love, either, in the look exchanged between aunt and nephew.

'What happened next?' asked Quy.

Mrs Flitcroft had asked Miss Lillah Keer if she would kindly allow her to return home via the mansard windows and the roof-gutter. It was a perfectly – well, *almost* perfectly – safe proceeding, and she and others had done it before. One had only to get out of the top window and walk along the gutter between the roof and the parapet. There was a narrow party wall of the same height as the parapet at the junction of the two houses, but there was plenty of room for a normally agile person to scramble over this without any danger of falling.

At this point, Inspector Quy asked to be conducted to the top floor so that he might judge for himself. He leant out of the small casement window of the bedroom, noted that the parapet was about two and a half feet high, and observed that the only obstacles to a walk along the gutter from end to end of the terrace were the low party walls between house and house. He also noted that a person travelling from Number 31 to Number 33 would have the roofs and the windows on his left hand.

'It certainly doesn't look very dangerous,' he commented.

'And it isn't!' said Miss Keer scornfully. 'Whatever that old fool Doctor Pellett may say! Poor Lillah *couldn't* have fallen! Somebody pushed her over!'

'How dare you?' said Mrs Flitcroft, in angry tears.

'Why didn't you go yourself, then? It was *you* who wanted to get home!'

Inspector Quy awaited with interest the answer to this question.

'Well, of course I meant to go myself!' replied Mrs Flitcroft tearfully. 'But I'd been out to tea and had my best things on, and Miss Keer was in her working clothes! It was very kind of her – she *insisted*!'

'So she came up here while you waited below for your nephew to open your door?'

'Well, no! I came up with her ...'

'Why?'

'Well, I still thought *I* ought to go: I didn't like imposing on her good nature!'

'So you actually *saw* her fall?'

'Well, no! I saw her get out of the window, but I didn't look to see what happened – I didn't think it *could* be dangerous, you see! I was looking at that picture – it's one of Peter's – and I heard her scream, and then I heard the thud ... And I rushed to the window, but of course I couldn't see over the parapet! I saw my nephew looking out of his window, and I told him what had happened, and we both rushed downstairs.'

'Who got there first?'

'I did,' said Mrs Flitcroft. And I put my coat over her, and when Peter came I went to telephone you. And then Miss Rachel Keer came home—'

'Yes, and oh! If only I'd been five minutes earlier! I wouldn't have let Lillah go! I'd have told this woman to go and sit on her doorstep! I tell you, Inspector, Lillah *didn't* fall accidentally! She was pushed off!'

'A push *might* be accidental,' said Inspector Quy. He paused, glancing from one to another, but no one spoke. Inviting Peter Crangley to accompany him, he climbed out of the window and walked along the gutter towards Number 33. It was obvious, from the scratches and rubbings on the sooty coping of the parapet, that Miss Lillah Keer had fallen while negotiating the party wall, the one point at which an accident would be possible. The sash-window of Peter Crangley's room was open at the bottom. Quy climbed into the comfortable bed-sitting-room, followed by its tenant.

'Was your window open when Miss Keer fell?'

'What, in this weather? No, I opened it when I heard her scream.'

Inspector Quy sniffed.

'Turpentine – but of course! You're an artist, too. You heard her scream, then? Although you had the wireless on?'

'Good God, yes!' Peter Crangley shuddered. 'I heard her scream. I switched off the wireless, and dashed to the window.'

'What programme was on? Just a routine question.'

'The Children's Hour.'

'And what was on the Children's Hour this evening? Just routine, you know.'

The young man laughed.

'I haven't the slightest idea! I wasn't really listening, just having the thing as a sort of background noise ...' He stopped rather suddenly.

'To what?' asked Quy quickly.

Peter Crangley hesitated.

'Not to housework, by any chance?' continued Quy.

'Housework!' The young man laughed awkwardly.

'Well, it has to be done,' said Quy seriously. 'Nothing for us men to be ashamed of, nowadays. I do lashings of it when I'm off-duty. Your place looks very nice and clean – nice polished floor. Who cleans it?'

'Well, as a matter of fact you're quite right, I do it myself,' confessed Peter Crangley. 'I can't afford a housemaid on the pay of a PO clerk, you know! And I haven't sold any pictures yet!'

'Where do you keep your brushes?' asked Quy.

'My brushes? In that jar there!' said the young man, staring.

Quy laughed.

'Not your paintbrushes – your housework brushes! But I suppose,' he added thoughtfully, 'you use a mop for a polished floor. My wife does.'

'It's in that cupboard,' said the young man, with a sudden odd hesitation.

Inspector Quy opened the cupboard door and took out a long-handled and very dirty floor mop. He sniffed at its pleasant scent of turpentine, and twirled it gently round, loosing a little air flotilla of fluff and motes into the room.

'Don't do that!' protested the young man agitatedly. He had gone very pale, and was blinking furiously.

'Not indoors, eh?' said Quy. 'No, one shouldn't. One should do it out of the window. I know, I've seen my wife do it.'

He took the mop to the window, thrust it through into the dark and twirled it over the parapet.

'That's what I meant when I said a push *might* be accidental,' he explained, desisting and returning the mop to its cupboard. 'It *might*, or it might not … Just as the window *might* have been open when the lady was coming along the gutter?'

'You don't think I'd try to hurt Lillah Keer, do you?' cried Peter Crangley in a strained, breathless voice. 'She was my best friend!'

Inspector Quy suggested gently:

'But it *might*, mightn't it, have been the *wrong lady* who was knocked over the parapet by the push that might have been accidental from the mop that might have been shaken out of the window that might have been open? I think, Mr Crangley, you'd better come with me to the police station. There are a few questions I'll have to ask you – not just routine, this time!'

The questions, which concerned the abstraction of a bunch of keys, before her departure, from Mrs Flitcroft's handbag, and the restoration of them to the pocket of a fur coat lying over a dead body, as well as certain other matters which soon came to light connected with Mr Crangley's ambition for an artist's career, and his share in a trust left by his grandfather, in which his aunt had a life interest, led eventually to the conviction of Peter Crangley for the murder of Lillah Keer, and, it is to be hoped, to apologies from Miss Rachel Keer to Mrs Flitcroft. It also led to reflections from Inspector James Quy on the inflexibility of the criminal mind.

'If young Crangley had accepted the fact that he had unfortunately killed the wrong lady, and had carried on with the perfectly sound scheme he'd thought out for the murder of his aunt, and simply left her keys in her bedroom or somewhere, and admitted at once that he'd shaken his floor mop out of the window just at the fateful moment, there'd almost certainly have been a verdict of accidental death. After all, a person doing housework on the top storey can't be expected to look out in the roof gutter to make sure the coast is clear before shaking a mop over it! But no, having killed the wrong lady, he had to pursue his obsession to get rid of his aunt by trying to fasten the murder of Miss Keer on her! Too rigid-minded. Must have their way at all hazards, these criminals. Can't cut their losses. And a good job for the rest of us, eh, Baker?'

PC Baker, who, although he has not made much of an appearance in this story, was a bright young officer, brightly agreed.

Credits

'Haunted House' by Gladys Mitchell is reprinted by permission of David Higham Associates on behalf of the Gladys Mitchell estate

'Sleuths on the Scent' by Dorothy L. Sayers is reprinted by permission of David Higham Associates on behalf of the Dorothy L. Sayers estate

'Meeting in the Snow' by Julian Symons is reprinted by permission of Curtis Brown Ltd, London, on behalf of the Literary Estate of Julian Symons. Copyright 1961 © Julian Symons

'The Reprisal' by Michael Innes is reprinted by permission of Peters, Fraser and Dunlop (www.petersfraserdunlop.com) on behalf of Rights Limited

While every effort has been made to contact copyright-holders of each story, the editor and publishers would be grateful for information where they have been unable to trace them, and would be glad to make amendments in further editions.